D0315024

Shades of Magenta

Other  titles

Magenta Orange
Magenta in the Pink
Magenta Goes Green
Magenta Sings the Blues
Mimosa Fortune
Blaggers
Diamond Geezers
Echo Freer

Bend it Like Beckham
Narinder Dhami

Guitar Girl
Sarra Manning

ECHO FREER

Hodder
Children's
Books

a division of Hachette Children's Books

I would like to thank the following people for their help and support: my husband Frank, for his insightful ideas-storming sessions; my wonderful children, Imogen, Verien and Jacob for their suggestions and advice; my agent, Caroline, and editor, Rachel, for their hard work and, of course, my late brother, Martin Freer Sunley, for getting himself into so many pickles when he was young. I'd also like to thank Shahazad Ahmed of Springfield Community School, for inspiring me with his story about a donkey when he went on holiday!

Text copyright © 2007 Echo Freer

First published in Great Britain in 2007
by Hodder Children's Books

1

ISBN-13: 978 0 340 94417 2

Typeset in Palatino by Avon DataSet Ltd,
Bidford-on-Avon, Warwickshire

Printed in the UK by CPI Bookmarque, Croydon, CR0 4TD

Hodder Children's Books
a division of Hachette Children's Books
338 Euston Road
London NW1 3BH

For Queen Vee, with love

1

Magenta

OK – when someone mentions the word *holiday* doesn't the image of blue skies, soft sand and sizzling Mediterranean sunshine spring to mind? I mean, I don't think I'm being totally unreasonable to expect that, after the year of trauma I've had, my dad could at least have booked somewhere just a teensy bit exotic for me to recharge my batteries. After all, Seema's going to Greece with her mum and dad and Arlette's family are off to Spain for two weeks.

For those of you who haven't managed to keep up with the programme, Seema and Arlette are my best mates – apart from Daniel, that is (who also happens to be the most gorgeous boyfriend in the entire universe – plus, he lives right next door to me, which is even better!). Our houses have balconies on the front and Daniel and I have bedrooms that are next to each other and open on to the balconies which means that we can just pop in and out of each other's rooms, or sit out and just chill and talk and all sorts of romantic things. Even when we've been told to go to bed, Daniel's turned his bed round so that his bed-head is against the same wall as mine and we can talk through the wall to each other. I mean, how thoughtful is that? Am I the luckiest girl in the world or what?

Well, in the boyfriend stakes, maybe, but don't even get me started on the holiday front. I mean, talk about hypocrisy – it's fine for my dad to take Belinda, his new wife, to Italy for their honeymoon. But where are they taking me for my summer holiday? Norfolk. *Norfolk!* Can you believe it? They go swanning off to soak up some Riviera rays but then drag me off to the North Sea for grey skies, grey sea and goose bumps!

And to make things a thousand times worse my entire extended family is going as well. I mean, my gran, Florence, is OK; she lives with us – well, strictly speaking, we live with her. Dad and I moved in after my mum died when I was three. But then there's Gran's sister, Auntie Venice (who, I swear, doesn't like me) and Dad's brother Uncle Wayne and his family: Auntie Heather (who's got a face like a smacked bum and is another who has it in for me) and the cousins from hell, Justine and Holden. Honestly, my family makes the Munsters look like the Brady Bunch.

'There! It's all booked!' From the way Dad tossed the Internet booking forms on to the table, it was like he expected a fanfare of trumpets to strike up. 'It wasn't easy finding somewhere that could accommodate all of us at such short notice, but we were lucky.'

'Lucky?' Hadn't it occurred to him that there was a reason they still had places available? Like no one wanted to go there – durr! I was staring in disbelief at the picture he'd printed out, which looked like somewhere that had been recently vacated by the army and hurriedly painted in pastel colours to try and make it look more attractive. 'I can't believe you're expecting me to go to this place – it's gross.'

'Magenta!' Don't get me wrong, as stepmothers go, Belinda's pretty cool. She's into love and peace and all that hippy stuff. She used to be my Art teacher but then she took the home–school liaison thing a bit far and married my dad. Now she seems to think she has the right to boss me about – as if! 'That's not very gracious, love, after all the trouble your dad's gone to, to try and arrange this.'

Oh great – all aboard for the Guilt Trip!

'Well, like it or not, Magenta, you're going and you *will* enjoy yourself.' My dad's always taken the Adolf Hitler approach to parenting. 'And you will not mention any of this to your grandmother – it's a surprise!'

Yeah, right! So much of a surprise she'll need a pacemaker when she finds out. It's Gran's seventieth birthday this year – five days before my fourteenth birthday actually. Which is so unfair, because I've been waiting all year for my fourteenth birthday and now dad's planning this mega extravaganza for Gran, so everyone'll be birthdayed out by the time it gets to mine.

'I remember when I was a child . . .' Uh-oh – I sensed a nostalgia moment coming on. Dad's head was tilted to one side and he was looking wistfully at the corner of the ceiling – either that or there was a humungous spider up there and he'd gone into shock. '. . . Mum always wanted to take us on a Harry Hay's Holiday but Dad would never agree . . .' Seems like Granddad Orange had the right idea if you ask me. '. . . so I thought it only fitting that Wayne and I should fulfil her dream and take *her* for her birthday treat.'

If he'd wanted to diversify into the wish fulfilment business, why didn't he choose something that wouldn't inflict misery on innocent people – like breakfast in bed? Or I've lost count of the number of times Gran's said, 'I wish you'd cut that lawn, Curtis!' I'm sure there's a whole host of other things he could've looked into apart from dragging us all off to Harry Hay's Holiday Camp.

But there is one bright spot in all this: Dad has said that Daniel can come with us. Mary, Daniel's mum, also remarried recently (must be something in the water) and she's going off to Scotland with her new husband to see his family, so Daniel's going to come with us! You see my dad can be human sometimes – although between you and me, I think it's Belinda's influence; before he met her, he made Vlad the Impaler look like a nice guy.

Those of you who've been paying attention will know that Daniel and I have been on and off more times than your average light switch, but right now we are so on. And it's amazingly, wonderfully, fantastically, zillion-watt brilliant! The L word has even been mentioned – and not just in a *love-thy-neighboury* sort of way either.

We were on the balcony this evening. Daniel had put some music on and the French windows were open. We were lying on his duvet that he'd spread out – I had told him that I didn't think it was hygienic because Mrs Pickles' cat, Geranium, had done unmentionable things out there, but he just

5

spread it out anyway and said, 'Who cares? As long as I'm with the girl I love, nothing matters.'

Wow! How *Lord of the Rings* was that? As you know, I'm as much a feminist as the next girl, but when a boy starts talking *lurve*-stuff like that, it makes me feel really valued and I go tingly all over.

So, we were lying on his duvet on the balcony. Daniel was playing with my hair and winding it round his fingers and I was doing a checklist of everything I needed to take on holiday tomorrow. It was only twelve hours to departure and, on a panic scale of one to ten, I was well into double figures.

'Can you believe that Dad put his foot down and said I'd got one new bikini and I didn't need any more? One won't be nearly enough and all the decent shops are closed now – except for the supermarkets, and there's no way I'd be seen dead in some nerdy economy-label swimsuit.'

Daniel was staring dreamily at the strands of hair he was working into a figure of eight round his fingers. 'What about that turquoise one you wore in the garden last year? You looked lovely in that.'

'Daniel!' I know he probably meant it as a compliment – which was very sweet – but, honestly! Anyone with any sense of fashion would have picked up on the glaringly obvious clue in the words *last year.* 'I can't wear that *this* year.'

He shrugged and carried on playing with my hair. 'Oh – have you grown out of it?'

'Er – noooooo!' Cheek! 'But it's so last season. Anyway, I suppose there'll be a shop on site, won't there? And I'll have to have some more flip-flops when we get there. My dad said I had to take the old ones but after everything they had to stand in when we went to camp, they're not going anywhere near my feet again – all sorts of things could be lurking in the rubber!'

Daniel and I had been on the school camping trip last term, and the experience had practically scarred me for life. In fact, when you think about it, it makes Dad's decision to make me go to a holiday camp so soon afterwards even more insensitive. You only have to mention the word *camp* and I have horrendous flashbacks – but that's a whole different story.

'Now, I've packed my denim miniskirt as well as my pink ra-ra skirt and the black one with sequins on it for going out in the evenings. And I've got two pairs of crop jeans – one with embroidery and one without – plus the gorgeous pink dress I bought for the school camp that I never got to wear because the evil Mrs Blobby made me take it out of my bag. I've put in about a dozen tops, so that I can mix and match – do you think that'll be enough? And what if it's freezing? I mean, you know what the North Sea's like even in August. How many jumpers should I take, do you think?'

Daniel was gazing at me with this gorgeous smile on his face. 'It doesn't matter what you take; you'd look lovely in anything.' Wow – see what I mean about him being the best boyfriend ever! I was just about to lean over and give him a huge kiss of gratitude, when he only went and spoiled it all. 'When are Justine and Holden arriving, or are we meeting them there?'

I was shocked. After the unfortunate episode in the February half-term when my she-devil of a cousin had tried to seduce Daniel away from me, I couldn't believe that he was even thinking of going down that road again.

'Daniel! How could you!'

I started to stand up to go back into my own bedroom but my hair was wrapped round Daniel's fingers and, as I pulled away from him, it tightened like a noose.

'Ooowwww!' I fell back down on the duvet. 'You nearly pulled my hair out, Daniel. Let go of me.'

'Hey – ease up,' he said, trying to untwist his finger. 'It wasn't intentional and it wasn't me who started getting all freaked out and jumping up at the mention of my cousin's name. I could just as easily have accused you of dislocating my finger, but I didn't.' Whoa! Snappy, or what?

'Yes, that's right, my hair just leaped up and started wrapping itself round Peter Pointer, did it? I don't think so. And, what's more . . .' It was proving more difficult than I'd thought to untangle myself from Daniel. My hair seemed to have knotted itself round his index and middle fingers and the tips were going a disturbing shade of blue – the tips of his fingers, that is, not my hair.

'I think you might need to cut it,' Daniel suggested.

OK, so expecting me to wear last year's clothes was one thing, but telling me to cut my hair was beyond the pale. Had he got no sense of haute coiffeur? Didn't he know that you can't go chopping off chunks of hair at one side without levelling it up at the other and that was the slippery slope to skinhead-dom. If I embarked on that route, before I knew it, I'd end up looking like my cousin Justine with her red spiky Goth look.

Or maybe that was Daniel's plan? Justine had

always had more than a passing resemblance to me until she went over to the dark side. Maybe Daniel was trying to turn me into a clone of her to satisfy his secret desire? Maybe he didn't love me for myself after all. Maybe he only loved me because I reminded him of his fantasy woman? Oh, this was awful!

I was just considering whether or not the current situation could justify amputation when, down below us, in the road right in front of my house, a monstrous great gas-guzzling four-by-four pulled up. And talk about *speak of the devil*! Who should get out but the subject of mine and Daniel's most recent little tiff, my conniving cousin herself; followed by her grubling brother and Uncle Wayne and Auntie Heather. Oh deep joy! As far as I was aware, they were supposed to be visiting Auntie Heather's sister this week and then meeting us at the barracks tomorrow.

'What's happening, Danno?' Justine called up, then slipped off her blue-tooth headset and added, 'Oh, I didn't see you there, Magenta. You OK?'

Gggggrrr!

Daniel sprang to his feet, almost wrenching my hair from its follicles. 'Hey, it's Justine! Let's go down and say hi.'

'Ow, ow, ow!' The way he pulled me to my feet and led me downstairs by the hair was definitely bordering on abuse.

So my last night before my week of torture with the Addams Family has been ruined on many counts:

1) Dad only went and volunteered me to share my bedroom with Justine tonight, which means that Daniel and I can't shout our goodnights to each other through the wall. I'm like: Durr! You arrived early, so it's not my problem that you've got nowhere to sleep tonight. Anyway, their car is larger than your average caravan – what's wrong with sleeping in that?

2) Justine has added a new word to her (very limited) vocabulary – *awesome*! Everything's, 'Oo, Daniel, your room's awesome this way round.' And, 'Have you seen my new mobile; it's awesome.' And, 'Dad's new car's really awesome.' Yawn, yawn, yawn. Bor-ing!

3) Belinda has had to cut Daniel's fingers out of my hair, which has made it so lopsided – I'll probably have to wear a wrap all week.

And,

4) Auntie Heather has only gone and put her spoke in about the sleeping arrangements next

week. I had it all planned: Dad, Belinda and I would have one of the twin-roomed chalets (in reality read: wooden huts), while Daniel slept on the bed-settee in the living room. Gran and Auntie Vee would share the studio apartment and the Freak Family would have the other chalet – simple! But Auntie Heather said it would make more sense for Daniel to share a room in their chalet with the brat, Holden, while Justine comes and shares with me!

And – just when things couldn't get any worse – all my friends are on holiday (and in so much better places than Harry Hay's!) so I'm being deprived of my entire support network too. Life is so unfair!

2
Daniel

I know I'm nearly fifteen now and this probably sounds really nerdy, but I could hardly sleep last night I was so excited about going away. OK, so it's not like I'm going to Ayia Napa with the lads, or anything like that, and I know there'll be loads of adults from Magenta's side with us, but even so, it's pretty cool to get away from my own family for a while. Mum's gone to Scotland with Donald, her new husband, and Joe, my gator-faced brother, is staying at Dad's. So this is the first time I've been on holiday without either of my parents – well, apart from school trips and a couple of times to cub camp when I was about Holden's age. So it's like I'm totally free for seven whole days.

And, even better – I'll be able to be with my beautiful Magenta twenty-four seven for the entire week. Or at least that *was* the plan – until Heather, Magenta's auntie, screwed things up on that score. She said it was 'immoral' for me to sleep on the bed-settee in Magenta's chalet. I didn't think anyone even used that word these days. So she's making me sleep in the same room as the poisonous pixie – aka her son. If you ask me, it's immoral making anyone share a room with that little brat.

But once I'd got my head round it, I worked out that if I allow seven hours for sleeping and half an hour for saying goodnight and another half an hour for waking up and getting ready, that still means I'll be with the love of my life *sixteen* seven – which, after all, is two thirds of twenty-four seven and sixty-six point six six recurring per cent is better than none – which is exactly how much time I'd be with her if I was staying at home and not going with them. So when you think about it, the positives of the holiday outweigh the negatives big time.

Curtis, Magenta's dad, had told me to be round at their house ready to set off by nine o'clock, which wasn't a problem because I'd been awake since five, partly with the excitement but also, that was the time Mum and Donald set off to Scotland. The trouble was, even though I was dressed, packed and eager to lock up and go round to Magenta's house, the maggot Holden was soundo. I'd already had to drag him off his camp-bed and almost carry him into the bathroom, but then he fell asleep again sitting on the toilet. Which, apart from being the worst sight ever, wasn't remotely surprising as he'd been up half the night telling me the most unfunny jokes I've ever heard:

'Hey, Daniel, how do you know if your cat's got a cold?'

'Go to sleep, you little toerag. It's turned midnight and I haven't got a cat.'

'Because it's got catarrh! Get it, cat-arrh?'

Even an imbecilic baboon would get it but I tried to humour him. 'Yes, I get it,' I groaned.

'You get it!' Followed by manic giggling. 'You get catarrh!' More lunatic laughter. 'You're snotty!' Snigger, snigger.

'Just go to sleep, you little squirt.' I pulled the pillow over my head to try and block out his voice.

'How about this one? Why is history called the Dark Ages?'

'You'll be history if you don't shut up!'

'Because it has so many knights!'

I was just about ready to leap out of bed and practise the Jackie Chan-style drop-kick I'd seen on Spud's DVD on him – that way I could put him out cold and drift off to dream of the best girlfriend in the whole world, free from his irritating interruptions. But just as I'd thrown off the duvet and adopted my ninja pose, there was a knock on my French window.

'OK, flea-face, you've been saved this time, but any more of your stupid jokes and I'm warning you . . .' I rolled up the blind expecting to see the wonderful vision of Magenta standing on the balcony, but instead I came face to face with her cousin, Justine.

'Huh? What are you doing here?' I asked, opening the window just wide enough to whisper at her. Then I poked my head out and looked along the balcony towards Magenta's window. 'Where's Magenta?'

Justine flapped her hand. 'Oh, she's out like a light but I couldn't sleep.'

'Me neither!' I confessed, trying not to glare too harshly at her idiot brother (who, by the way, looked even more like a maggot than usual curled up in his brown sleeping bag).

'Can I come in?' she asked. 'It's a bit chilly out here.'

'Erm . . .' I only sleep in my shorts and a basketball vest, so I was hardly dressed for receiving visitors – but I didn't know what to say without offending her. 'OK then.'

'Awesome!' and she was through the French window and curled up on my bed before I could say New York Knicks.

'So . . . er . . . what's happening?' I said, retrieving my duvet and pulling it over me to make myself decent.

Justine gave a casual shrug. 'Nothing. Just thought I'd pop round and see what was happening over here.' Then the ratfink in the camp-bed started making these gross, slobbery kissing noises. Justine leaned over and grabbed her brother by the pyjama jacket. 'Pack it in, grub-gob!' She pulled his face right up to hers and snarled, 'Or that noise will be the only one you can make for the rest of the holiday. Get it?'

Whoa! Justine can be very forceful when she wants to be. A bit too forceful, if I'm being honest. 'Look, Juss, it's probably best if you go back and let me get some sleep,' I said, trying to put it in a way that wouldn't upset her.

She shrugged. 'I thought you said you *couldn't* sleep?'

Who was she; the human polygraph? 'Well, I couldn't but—' I was just about to launch into an explanation about having to get up at five to see Mum and Donald off when she moved right up to me and started running her fingers over the Nike logo on my basketball vest.

'Wow, Daniel, have you been working out since I last saw you?'

Eeek! Don't get me wrong: it was pretty flattering that she'd noticed my improved upper body strength (and it proved that breaking my leg and having to be on crutches for so long did have advantages), but running her hands over my chest in the middle of the night was way too full on. I started to back away. 'Look . . . er . . . Mum's trusting me to lock up and everything tomorrow, so . . . er . . . I need to be alert and . . . er . . . well, I think it's just best if you . . .'

'Jeez, relax.' She dropped her hand and gave a whispery laugh. 'I'm only winding you up.'

Phew! She stood up and I thought she was going to leave but instead she leaned over me and was just about to bang on the wall above my head. 'Shall we try and wake Magenta up and see if she wants to come over and join us?'

Did she have a death-wish? Or did she just not know Magenta at all? I mean, Magenta's really sweet and trusting and everything, but she can also be very insecure at times. The last thing I wanted was for her to get the wrong idea –

especially after the last time Justine came down to stay. 'Durrr – no!'

'Oh go on.' Justine had her fist poised about five centimetres away from the wall and was smiling at me with one of those *don't-be-such-a-cowardy-custard* expressions.

'No really – I don't want you waking up Mum and Donald.' Nicely hedged, I thought.

She shrugged. 'OK, see you tomorrow then, scaredy-cat.' And, as she disappeared out of my French window, she turned and blew me a kiss.

I flopped back on my bed and I don't mind admitting, talk about confused.com! My mind was doing about a thousand revs per minute trying to work out what had just happened. Then Holden puckered up again and started making his disgusting sound effects that were supposed to be kissing noises.

'Leave it out,' I snapped, lobbing my pillow at him.

'She fancies you,' he said, dodging out of the way – amazingly skilfully, actually, for a nine-year-old with no brain.

'Yeah right!'

'OK, don't believe me, then.' He lay down, then whispered, 'But I got an electronics kit for my birthday and I've bugged her bedroom, so I can listen to all her phone calls.'

'What! That's despicable.'

He propped himself up on one elbow. 'Hey – d'you want me to show you how to wire up Magenta's room so you can . . .'

'Ewww – no! Don't you know anything about *The Human Rights Act*?' Why was I even asking? Of course he didn't – he'd have to be human to have even heard of it, let alone abide by it, and Holden was still in the Cretaceous period of evolution. I retrieved my pillow and rolled over so that my back was to him. 'And anyway, shouldn't you have turned into a pumpkin by now?'

There was silence for about a millisecond and I thought, a little too optimistically as it turns out, that he'd dozed off.

But then, 'Daniel, what do prehistoric monsters do when they're asleep?'

It would've been nice if one particular prehistoric monster would actually go to sleep but that was one joke too many; it was time to exercise my six years' seniority over the little mutant. 'Shut it! I don't want another word out of you or I'll . . .' Uh-oh! I wasn't sure what sanctions I could mete out that would have the slightest impact on him . . . but I knew someone who would. '. . . or I'll call Justine back in here.' OK, I know it wasn't very manly of me to threaten him with a girl, but let's face it, his sister had way more effect on him than I ever had.

'No way!' And I didn't hear another peep out of him all night – mission accomplished.

But although Holden might have gone off to sleep, I was still wide awake. I didn't know if the nerd had been winding me up but the thought that Justine might actually fancy me was going round and round my head like one of those annoying little flies that you can't swat. I mean she's really funny and cool and everything, and I know we sort of went out at Curtis's fortieth birthday party last February, but that was only because Magenta and I were on a break and Justine was on her own. It wasn't serious. And it's not like *I* fancy *her*. She's into this Goth look at the moment, which just doesn't do it for me. One of the (many) things I love about Magenta is the way she's so natural and lovely, exactly the way she is. OK, so she runs glitter through her hair to give it that extra little sparkle, which is really sweet. And sometimes she puts that blue stuff on her eyelids and every now and then her lips taste like cherry bubblegum and have an extra shimmer to them. But apart from that, she's just got natural beauty. Whereas her cousin uses all that punky purple lipstick with loads of black round her eyes. She reminds me of when I was about twelve and Dad took Joe and me to watch *The Rocky Horror Show* as a Christmas treat. It was a bit weird if I'm being honest – except that there was one character called Magenta (although she wasn't a patch on my Magenta). But whenever I see Justine with all her make-up on, there's a part of me wants to burst into song with, 'Let's do the time warp aga-ain!'

So Holden's most recent revelation had really messed with my mind and the person I'd usually turn to for all my relationship advice was just about to go roaming in the gloaming for a week. I knew I had to act fast before she left.

'So you see, I don't fancy her at all. But Holden says that *she* fancies *me* and I don't want Magenta to get the wrong idea and think there's anything going on because she might get upset and that'll ruin the holiday and I don't know what to do about it because—'

'Daniel!' Mum was standing in front of me with her jacket over her arm and a key in her hand, looking a tad tetchy, I have to say. I know it was five a.m. but she could've shown a little bit of concern for her son's problems before she went off and left me for a whole week. 'We've talked about integrity before and Donald and I really need to be getting going. Now if you've changed your mind and don't want to go away with Curtis . . .'

Whoa! Why do parents do that? They take one small thing and magnify it to the hundredth degree. 'No, I *do* want to go. I really do.'

'Good. Then you just have to state your truth, Daniel, and don't get drawn into other people's dramas.' Yeah, Mum – great theory, now a little insight into how to put it into practice would go down a treat. My mum has more self-help books than your average library but all the books in the world are useless if she doesn't help me out with a practical solution to my dilemma. 'So, when you and Holden have finished here, check all the windows are shut and locked, all the taps are off and the back door's bolted. Then lock the front door and leave the keys at Florence's. I don't want you losing them somewhere in Norfolk.' I nodded in the mature way that I thought reflected the responsibility she was showing me. I mean, it was a pretty big thing to be left in charge of a house *and* a nine-year-old at my age and I wanted Mum to know that she could trust me one hundred and ten per cent. 'Now reception's pretty poor where

Donald's daughter lives, so this is her landline.' She handed me a piece of paper. 'But don't call me unless it's a life and death emergency; it's about an eight-hour drive.'

I folded up the paper and stuffed it into my shorts pocket with the intention of putting it into my address book later. 'OK. Have a good trip and don't worry about a thing,' I reassured her.

So, I'd had four hours to shower and get myself ready but now the nine o'clock deadline was rapidly approaching and the little brat was holding everything up. I'm not a believer in physical violence but right at that moment, Holden was testing my principles to the max.

I went into the bathroom for the fourth time and saw him still slumped on the bog with his toothbrush hanging out of his mouth (gross), so I lifted his head up and slapped a wet flannel across his face. 'If you don't wake up and get yourself dressed, I'll go and fetch the girls to do it for you.' That brought some life into the evil weevil. 'OK – now I'm going next door to get some breakfast and when I come back to lock up, I want you out of here – understood?'

There was a grunt that I took for a 'yes'.

So, let me go through my final checklist:

1. Get the grub out of the house – which is in process – sort of.
2. Make sure all the windows are shut and locked – check! I'd done that in between playing PS2 while I'd been waiting for the rest of the world to wake up – except for the French window in my room because I need that to access Magenta's house – obviously.
3. Lock back door – check! Accomplished between O five hundred hours and now.
4. And finally, lock the front door and leave the key next door – once the house has been certified an insect-free zone of course.

OK – we are ready to rumble! Let me get round there and see my wonderful Magenta again. This is going to be a holiday of a lifetime.

3
Magenta

Honestly! In the time it took the Orange Family Circus to get on the road, most people could have been halfway across Europe. Although, with hindsight (which Auntie Heather seems to have in abundance!), it might have been better if we'd never set off in the first place.

But I'm getting ahead of myself because, before we'd even got as far as loading up the convoy, my senses had had to contend with so many assaults, I'm surprised I hadn't gone blind and deaf:

1. First of all, I woke up to see Justine – which would have been enough of a shock to my system on its own, but she was sitting in front of my mirror with so much eye make-up on, she looked like an exhibit in Beijing Zoo. Plus she was plastering her lips with the sort of purple poster paint I used to use in nursery school. Doesn't the word 'subtle' feature *anywhere* in her vocabulary?

2. Then, when I tried to escape from one truly gruesome sight that was polluting my bedroom,

I was met with an equally shocking one clogging up the landing: Auntie Heather was flapping about in the most disgustingly floral dressing gown ever to escape from a nineteen-seventies jumble sale. But even more scary was the fact that her hair seemed to have morphed into multicoloured curly fries and they were popping out all over her head.

3. And it didn't end there. I ventured down to the kitchen, in the hope that breakfast might settle my stomach, only to find Uncle Wayne in stars and stripes boxer shorts (pul-lease – has he no pride?) waving a grill pan of burned toast that was pumping out clouds of evil smoke everywhere.

4. And, just in case you think that the whole Ministry of Mayhem antics were down to the Freak side of the family, my dad was wearing some of Belinda's tie-dye yoga trousers that were about six sizes too small for him and scurrying about under the table trying to grab hold of our dog, Sirius, so that he could take him across the road to Mrs Pickles' while we're away.

And, as if my eyes weren't suffering enough from all the gross visual images, my ears hadn't gone totally unscathed either:

5. Uncle Wayne's attempt at doing a Jamie Oliver had resulted in both upstairs and downstairs smoke alarms going off – simultaneously, but not quite synchronised – causing serious ear-al damage.

6. Auntie Heather was ranting on about Uncle Wayne's culinary (and general) uselessness and the fact that we only had one bathroom (ex-cuse-me!) at about a thousand decibels – yawn, yawn, yawn – put another record on – all she ever does is moan.

7. Justine had commandeered my hi-fi and the music that was thumping out of my room had me grabbing for the sick bag. I just hope that no one thought it was *my* taste.

Finally, as if all that wasn't enough to make me want to put myself up for adoption, and while we're on the subject of sick bags . . .

8. Belinda had eaten a dodgy vegetable korma last night and, oh my days, wasn't she letting everyone know about it. (Which, by the way, was Auntie Heather's number one argument for a downstairs cloakroom.)

But by far the most shocking thing to be inflicted on my very delicate nature this morning happened when I was on my way back up to my room.

'Hi de hi!' Gran leaped out of her bedroom into the middle of the landing and I could not believe what I was seeing. I mean, the catchphrase is bad enough but I've sort of got used to that now. After all, she's been shouting it like a mantra ever since Dad and Uncle Wayne broke the news of the holiday to her last night. But as for what she was wearing . . . Oh! My! God! 'What do you think, love? Isn't it gorgeous? It's an early birthday present from Venice. We saw it in the bike shop in the High Street a couple of months ago and I fell in love with it. Vee's been keeping it as a surprise ever since. Don't I have the best sister in the world?'

My gran always runs her sentences into one without giving anyone else a chance to get a word in, but this time I was grateful; the more she rambled on, the more time I had to come out of shock.

Picture (if your imagination stretches that far – and if your stomach can bear it) a seventy-year-old (well, almost – give or take a few days), twirling round and round in a scarlet – yes, SCARLET! – leather catsuit! Not a pretty sight, is it? But add to that more ironmongery than your average DIY superstore and you'll have a pretty good image of the vision that confronted me as I reached the top of the stairs. Think: Speedway meets ZZ Top – except that Gran doesn't have a beard like ZZ Top (well, not unless you stood her on her head, in which case her mad hair might look a bit like a beard). And she was dripping with chains that flared out as she spun round. But the worst bit was, when she stopped her Whirling Dervish act and stood still, she turned her back to me and across her shoulders, in an arc of studwork, were the words *Go Flo*. Could she be any more embarrassing?

'I can't wait to show the others. Hi de hi!' she said, heading downstairs for the kitchen.

Seriously – I cannot believe I'm related to these people. I decided that I needed to get out of that environment and go next door to find Daniel – and, hopefully, sanity. But, when I opened my bedroom door, can you believe it – he was already in there! And he was only sitting on *my* bed talking to Justine – before he'd even come to say hello to me!

'Hi, beautiful!' he oiled, standing up and walking towards me as though he was going to get a kiss. Yeah right! If that wasn't the talk of a guilty conscience, I don't know what was. What I wanted to know, though, was what was he feeling guilty about?

'Don't *beautiful* me,' I said. 'What are you doing here?'

He stopped and his eyes did this sort of sideways flicker. 'Erm . . . because we're going on holiday today?'

'Durr – I know *that*. I mean, what are you doing in here? With . . .' I caught Justine's eye through the mirror.

'Oh, don't mind me, Magenta. Daniel and I were just catching up.' She gave me this really knowing grin so that I *knew* they'd been up to something. Then she looked at Daniel and added, 'Weren't we, Danno?'

Gggrr! I hate it when she calls him that. It's OK for Daniel's boy mates to call him Danno, but she's a girl and she shouldn't be trying to muscle in on something that's so obviously a boy thing – it's against the laws of nature. I was just about to tell her as much when there was a knock on my bedroom door – which was very respectful, I thought. But, before I could answer it, Auntie Heather walked straight in – which wasn't remotely respectful!

'I thought I heard your voice, Daniel.' She was peering round my room with her nose in this permanent *bad-smell* expression, as though she was trying to locate something that had died about a week ago. I wouldn't mind, but there were only two things in the room that were dead and they both belonged to her:

1) her daughter's brain cell and
2) her own fashion sense; I was praying she was still wearing her pyjamas because the unspeakable alternative was that she was going to go out of the house in that outfit. Really – those trousers and top should never have been released on to the High Street; they were obviously straight out of the clown shop.

'Holden?' she said, as she wandered into my room with her neck sticking out like some sort of sniffer giraffe. 'Darling?'

'Oh, he's not here, Mrs Orange,' Daniel said. 'I just popped over for some breakfast while I'm waiting for him to have a wash.'

'WHAAAAAAAT!' Auntie Heather was across my room like an Olympic long jumper, pushing Daniel back towards the French window. 'Get back in there, you stupid boy!' Whoa – and this coming from the woman who was dressed like a sideshow freak? 'How dare you leave him alone in there?'

'Sorry, I'll just . . .' Poor Daniel looked soooo upset. I was torn – part of me just wanted to go over there and give him a big hug but the other part was still a bit peed off that he'd stayed talking to Justine instead of coming to find me.

And then Justine decided to get in on the Daniel-bashing act as well. 'Get real, Danno – if you're waiting for Holden to get washed, we'll be here till Christmas. He hasn't been near water for months. Personally, I think he's got rabies.'

Who did Justine think she was, talking to my boyfriend like that? Although, on the positive side, it probably meant that nothing had been going on between the two of them after all, which was a relief. Or, wait a minute . . . it could mean that she was trying to double bluff me to throw me off the scent! Now I come to think of it – that was so obviously what was going on. I can't believe I'd been so blind. I glared at her through the mirror and she smacked her lips together, sealing her purple lipstick, then gave me a smile like the bride of Dracula.

'That's not necessary, Justine!' Auntie Heather snapped.

Justine shrugged. 'Maybe not necessary, but true.'

'I'm really sorry. I didn't mean . . .' Daniel was squirming – which served him right for flirting with my cousin the minute I turned my back.

He was just about to go back over the balcony to get Holden, when the little nerd himself

33

appeared at the French window with white stuff smeared all round his lower face – which meant that either he couldn't even hit home with a toothbrush, or that Justine was right and he was foaming at the mouth with rabies. 'Is breakfast ready? I'm starving.'

Auntie Heather threw her arms round him as if he'd just been washed up after a year at sea. 'My poor darling! Let's go and get you something to eat,' she said, wiping the gunk off his chin. Then she turned on Daniel again. 'I think you'd better go and lock up and I hope you're not going to behave as irresponsibly as this on holiday, young man, or you and I shall be falling out.'

I must admit I was starting to feel a teensy bit sorry for Daniel. He had the sort of look on his face that Sirius puts on when he wants me to drop him some dinner under the table without Dad seeing. But I wasn't going to weaken. There was no way I was going to let Daniel think he could get away with it a second time.

'I need you to get out now, Daniel, so that I can repack my case,' I said, when the others had gone.

'But . . .'

'I'll see you downstairs,' I said, staying very aloof.

* * *

And that set the tone for the rest of the morning really; Daniel and I hardly spoke. Of course Justine made the most of it and was giggling and fluttering and flicking her hair whenever she saw him – and making a total fool of herself if I'm being honest. And by the time the cars were loaded up, it was almost lunch time and the temperature in Dad's old rust bucket was enough to bake biscuits.

'Sure you don't want to come with us, Danno?' Justine asked. 'Dad's new car's got awesome air con.'

Ggggrrr! 'No, actually, Justine, Daniel's fine to come with *us*,' I said.

And then Daniel started getting all macho again. 'I can speak for myself you know, Magenta.'

Wooooooo! Get him! 'Fine. Go with Justine, then.' See if I cared. This holiday already sucked and we hadn't even set off yet.

'Thanks, Juss, but I want to go with Magenta,' he said.

Then he picked up my hand, squeezed it and smiled at me. You see – guilt, written all over him. Well, if he thought he could get round me with a squeeze of the hand, he could think again. I got into the back seat, behind Belinda, strapped on my seat belt and wound down the window to try and bring the temperature down to something that wouldn't roast a turkey.

Belinda handed me the *Atlas of the British Isles*. 'If you wouldn't mind, Magenta, love, I don't think I'm up to map-reading – it always makes me feel queasy at the best of times.'

Oh, brilliant! Didn't she see my Geography results this year?

Dad started up the engine. 'I'm going to get Environmental Health on to that restaurant when we get back. They have no right serving up takeaway salmonella like that.'

'Leave it, Curtis!' Belinda snapped, putting her hand up in a *face-ain't-listening* sort of way. Uh-oh – looked like the beginnings of a domestic to me. Great – Daniel and I weren't talking in the back and now Dad and Belinda weren't talking in the front. Happy families!

Dad had agreed to lead the way on the basis that his road map was newer than Uncle Wayne's – taking no account of who was going to be reading it, of course. But you watch: I bet Auntie Heather stops off at the first garage to buy a more up to date one than us – she can't bear to think that we might have something better than her. Although, on the positive side, at least that would mean that she could take

36

over as navigator, which would be a huge weight off my shoulders.

Following us were going to be Gran and Auntie Vee on the biddy-bike – with the *awesome* foursome bringing up the rear in their obscene, environmentally *un*friendly turbo-tractor.

'Wagons roll!' Gran yelled from somewhere inside her grotesque biker's suit. 'Hi de hi!'

And the Orange convoy rumbled into gear. Great – this had all the makings of the worst holiday since holidays began! I stared down at the enormous book that Belinda had given me. At least it gave me something to focus on other than Daniel, who was sulking next to me. Although what I was supposed to do with it was beyond me – I was already having flashbacks to the orienteering section of the school's summer camp! I opened up the atlas at a random page and stared at something that bore a horrible resemblance to old Mrs Pickles' legs when she waters her pot plants in a swimming costume – red and blue lines running everywhere. Oh boy! At this rate, we'd be lucky to get to Harry Hay's Holiday Camp by next week – although, if the Internet pictures were anything to go by, that might not be such a bad thing. We can but hope.

4
Daniel

I know I've said it before and I'll probably say it about a thousand times more but I just do not know where girls are coming from. How their brains work is a Nobel prize-winning, da Vinci Code-cracking mystery that would melt the mind of the brainiest brainiac in the world.

Take Magenta – (I don't mean literally; I love her so much that when I don't see her even for a short time, it's like some medieval implement of torture has been rammed into my heart and twisted full circle about a thousand times, so there's no way I'd want anyone to *actually* take her, but you know what I mean) – when we're together, one minute everything's great, then the next I seem to do something that really pisses her off and it goes horribly pear-shaped. And you might be saying to yourself *well just stop doing the things that piss her off, Danno* – but how can I when I don't know what it is that I keep doing?

Yesterday, for example – we were all loved up and looking forward to this holiday, right? Then, bosh!

Her cousin turns up and Magenta morphs into some sort of hormonal hell hag, stomping around and slamming doors and sulking. And it seems to be *my* fault! I've been over it and over it in my head and, call me deluded, but I just cannot work out how. OK, I can understand that she might have been a bit jealous a while back, because Justine and I had a bit of a thing at her dad's birthday, but that was months ago. And since then, she's been out with my best mate, Spud, but do I hold it against her? No way!

Personally, I think she reads way too many magazine problem pages. She gets it into her head that all the problems somehow relate to her and her life. I'm like, *durrr! No one could be* that *dysfunctional!* But then she gets annoyed and says that I'm not taking her seriously. I can't win. It's like this whole thing with me and Justine; it doesn't matter how many times I've told her that it's a load of crap and nothing's going on, she just doesn't believe me. Her mind's taken one pathetic evening of loneliness on my part and made it into the love story of the millennium.

I mean, this morning, I was like a little kid I was so excited about going away with her. I'd been awake half the night, thinking about some of the wonderful things we could do together, like going for romantic walks on the beach by moonlight and maybe taking her out on the boating lake so that she'll be blown away by my newly toned biceps. I know she's seen my muscles in T-shirts and vests and stuff when we hang out together, but I was thinking that if she sees me in action, pulling on the oars of a rowing boat while she lies back and daintily trails her hand in the water, she'll be well impressed.

So you can imagine that when the time came for me to go round there and see her, I was really stoked. Even when Justine said Magenta had gone to the toilet and would be back in a minute, I didn't think there was anything to worry about. Everyone needs to take a leak now and then; nothing out of the ordinary there, is there? So I sat down on her bed to wait – perfectly innocent, right? Wrong!

Apparently, I should've gone looking for her. And, I'm thinking – *in the toilet? How does that work?* But, before I could even check it out with her, her maniac auntie started screaming at me for leaving her evil offspring on his own for five minutes. Five minutes! To be honest, if you left Holden on his own on top of Everest for a year, he'd probably come back to base camp cracking jokes about yetis up there having 'high tea'. I wouldn't mind but he was only in our bathroom; it wasn't like I'd left him in an explosives factory – more's the pity. But, while Heather was shooting her mouth off at me, did my girlfriend come to my assistance? I don't think so! She just stood there with her arms folded in that horrible *serves-you-right* sort of way. And for what? I hadn't done anything to be served right about!

Even after my tongue-lashing from her auntie, I was still hoping Magenta would go back home with me to lock everything up. But again – it ain't happening. In fact, she practically pushed me out of her French windows herself. Luckily it only took me a couple of minutes because I'd gone through my checklist about ten times already; all that was left for me to do was lock my bedroom windows and the front door then take my bag round to hers. And I was praying that Magenta might be in a better mood by the time I got round there – not that I'm really into praying but everybody needs a bit of help now and then, don't they? But I might as well have been rent-a-ghost for all the attention Magenta paid me. Whenever I spoke, she was all, 'Oh, did someone say something?'

So I spent the morning sitting on the bottom stair twiddling with my luggage label while Magenta's family ran around me like headless chickens and

Holden the Horrible fired his rubbish jokes at me. Magenta shut herself in her room to repack her case – five times! But the most annoying thing was that Justine kept coming up to me and rambling on about how cool it was going to be, all of us going away together.

'Hey, Danno, it'll be wicked going down the flumes with you in Waterworld. I've seen them on TV and they are totally awesome.'

'Brilliant,' I said, with about as much conviction as if she'd told me that we were going to be spending the week breaking rocks in Death Valley.

And the truth is, I didn't want to go down the flume with Justine. The only person I want to go down a flume, or a tunnel of love or even just the bog-standard, boring old garden path with, is Magenta. But the chances of that happening were slipping further and further into the abyss of hopelessness every time Magenta came downstairs, because her flipping cousin, Justine, was always talking to me. And she was laughing in that exaggerated flirty way she has where she throws her head back like a hyena on laughing gas. I mean, doesn't Magenta realise that I can see straight through her cousin? Justine is a teaser – plain and simple. But my poor native Magenta is so innocent herself that she doesn't realise her cousin's trying to wind us both up. And she keeps letting it get to her. If she'd only speak to me, I could explain. But right now, she's about as approachable as a top security no-go area.

So you can see that by the time we finally loaded the cars and set off, I was feeling pretty fed up. I felt less like I was going on holiday for a week and more like I'd been sent to Coventry for eternity. And as if it wasn't bad enough that I was feeling all hot under the collar because of Magenta, to make matters worse, it was turning out to be the hottest day of the summer. I've never actually been near a smelting furnace – you know, those massive oven things that melt iron; although I did see one once on a 'History of Steel' video in primary school, where men were shovelling coal into about a thousand degrees of heat – but on the scale of comfortable places to be sitting, Curtis's car today must have come pretty close to one of those bad boys; it was unbearable. As soon as we got in there, the sweat started to pour down my face like I'd just done ten circuits in the gym. And you couldn't let your skin touch the car seat in case you melted into the plastic. Even the handles that wind the windows practically blistered my hand. At least I had my cropped cargo pants on to protect my legs; poor Magenta was only wearing a little short skirt and she kept rocking from one side to the other, it was so hot. She looked so sweet.

'If you want, I can get one of my T-shirts out of my bag for you to sit on,' I offered.

'I'll be fine, thank you,' she said, leaning so far away from me she was practically hanging out of the window.

You see – it doesn't matter what I say, it's wrong. I let out a big sigh and turned round to look at Justine and her family, all cool and calm with their air conditioning. I'm not proud of this you understand, but I did have a twinge of regret over my decision not to go with them. At the time I'd been hoping for some sort of truce with Magenta, but I was beginning to realise that that wasn't going to be happening any time soon. I sat back and got out my PSP.

Before we'd set off, the dads had had a discussion about who should lead the way and they agreed that Curtis should go first – something to do with the hobgoblin tearing out several crucial pages from Wayne's road atlas and making paper darts to throw at passing motorists. But, reading between the lines, I think that was a load of BS; I think Wayne was just trying not to hurt Curtis's feelings because, to be honest, I don't think any of us trusted Curtis's junk-mobile to actually go the distance. To make matters worse, last week a van had rammed into the back of it and smashed up his boot. Now, not only was his car clapped-out but it was held together with gaffer tape. So it was a dent to his pride as well as his bumper when his brother rolled up in a brand new SUV. I really felt for the bloke. He's an OK guy is Curtis.

The two old biddies were going to be a sort of Kawasaki sandwich between the two cars; Florence won the toss and was driving, so Venice was riding pillion. I must say, if awards were being given out for eccentricity, I think those two would win it hands down. I wish my nan was as cool as Florence – she rocks! All my nan does is bake cakes and watch *Countdown* on daytime telly.

So there I was, feeling about as comfortable as a snowman in the Sahara, when Belinda handed the atlas over and asked Magenta to map-read. Personally, I've never really believed in premonitions and all that psychic stuff, but right then, I got this feeling in my gut that that was a really bad move. Don't get me wrong, Magenta has many talents – but map-reading is definitely not one of them. Granted, Belinda looked like something out of *Night of the Living Dead*, but even so, she could have asked me to do it. I don't want to brag or anything but I did get level six for Geography and our group did win the prize for the best orienteering exercise at camp.

For one stupid moment I thought I might try and use the opportunity to get back in Magenta's good books. 'Would you like me to do it for you?' I asked.

But she was persisting with her impersonation of the Polar Ice Cap. 'I'm fine, thank you, Daniel,' she said, opening up the book and peering at it like it was some amazingly interesting gossip column.

If the temperature in the car was the equivalent to the centre of the sun; the atmosphere between us was like the Tundra. And it didn't matter how hard I tried, I never seemed to get below the surface and penetrate the three metres of permafrost that Magenta had surrounded herself with. In the end, I put on my headphones and turned back to my PlayStation.

And in fact, it was a tactic that worked because I'd been so engrossed in fighting the forces of evil that, when I looked up, we'd left the motorway behind and the countryside was all fields and villages. We'd been driving for about a couple of hours and when I glanced across at Magenta, she was sitting with her head back and her eyes closed. She looked so beautiful, with her little turned-up nose and her gorgeous eye-lashes. And I love the shape of her chin – in fact I love everything about her – except maybe the fact that the road map was shut on her lap. I've navigated for Mum loads of times and I know how important it is to keep an eye on where we are.

The car slowed down as we approached a set of traffic lights on the outskirts of some little market town. There was a big green road sign but someone had graffitied over it so that it was impossible to tell one destination from another. I leaned across and tapped Magenta on the arm.

'What!' she hissed at me. 'I'm not asleep, you know.' So my theory that her grumpy mood was down to sleep deprivation went right out of the window.

'Which way here, love?' Curtis called over his shoulder to the back seat. It was good to see that at least he and Belinda seemed to have made up.

The car came to a stop and Magenta hurriedly opened the book of maps. 'Erm . . .'

She was running her finger all over the page and biting her bottom lip – she looks so cute when she does that.

'It's upside down,' I whispered, leaning over to help her turn it round.

But she pulled it away. 'I can manage, thank you.'

The lights turned to green and a car horn sounded from somewhere behind Wayne's massive motor, then another, then another till it sounded a bit like a chorus from 'Colonel Bogey'.

'Quickly!' Curtis snapped. 'We're holding everyone up.'

Magenta was still looking like she was staring at a map of Mars, so I tried again.

'You're on the wrong page,' I said quietly.

'Durrr!' She didn't even look at me when she spoke. 'I'm not stupid, you know. I'm just looking at . . . where we're . . . going to go next.'

I thought it might be better if I kept quiet about the fact that she had it open at Cornwall because as the car horns rose to a crescendo, Curtis was getting more and more flustered.

'Come on!' he shouted, tapping his fingers on the wheel.

Just at the point when I thought the big vein in his forehead was about to pop, there was a throbbing of an engine and a red leather arm appeared next to Magenta's open window. Florence and Venice pulled up alongside and Florence was shouting something from inside her crash helmet – not that any of us could make out what she was saying, because her visor was down. But she was doing some sort of weird semaphore-type hand movements and then seemed to be indicating straight ahead. Magenta gave her gran the thumbs-up.

'Straight on,' she said confidently.

A bit too late though, because the lights had gone to red again and the temperature in the car had gone up about another ten degrees. Curtis nudged forwards for a quick getaway, but there was a bang on the side of the car that made us all jump about a metre off our seats.

'What the . . .!' Curtis yelled. Florence was gesticulating wildly by the side of the car and Curtis groaned. 'Silly old fool!' He turned to Belinda. 'Find out what's the matter will you? I thought something had hit us again.' The lights changed to green and he started to pull away, still muttering about his mother. 'This trip might be her birthday treat, but she'd better not have done any more damage . . .'

'It'll be fine,' Belinda said, calmly. 'What damage can an old lady in thick leather biking gloves do to this car?'

Curtis changed up a gear and glanced across at

her. 'This isn't any old lady, you know – this is my mother we're talking about.'

Belinda smiled and nodded. 'True.'

We were picking up speed and heading for the town centre, where there seemed to be some sort of street market taking place. Uh-oh! I was getting the distinct impression that poor Magenta had taken us down a wrong turning back there and we'd ended up in car-free zone. Apart from an ice cream van, there wasn't another vehicle to be seen.

It was when I turned round to see if Wayne was still following us that I noticed Florence's red arm was still right up against Magenta's window and she was waving furiously as though she was trying to flag Curtis down.

'Hi, Gran!' Magenta called, waving back.

'What's going on?' Curtis asked. 'Should we have turned off or something? Magenta – check if we're on the right road.'

'Erm . . .' Magenta was flipping through the pages.

Florence and Venice were still right alongside us, and now they were both flapping their hands and trying to bang on the car roof. A man stepped out from the side of the road and seemed to be pointing at something on Curtis's car. I hoped he hadn't got a flat tyre.

'Get out of the road!' Curtis yelled at the man. He was clearly getting agitated. 'What is my mother trying to do? The silly idiot!' he said, giving a glance in his passenger-side wing mirror at the two old ladies straddling the Kawasaki 850. 'I know she doesn't want to get old, but it's like she's got some sort of death wish. And to be perfectly frank, whether she likes the idea of being seventy or not, I think the least she can do is hang on till after the holiday now that I've paid for it!'

'Curtis!' Belinda chastised, gently. 'That's not very nice.'

'Well!' he puffed. 'What is she trying to prove, sneaking up on the inside like that? Can't she see how dangerous it is with all these people?'

'I think maybe she's trying to tell you to turn round,' Belinda suggested. By this time we were crawling down the middle of the road with stalls on either side; some with clothes, others with toys, bags or toiletries. 'Oh, look at those candles,' Belinda went on, completely distracted. 'I wouldn't mind stopping and having a look if we've got time.'

People were shaking their arms at us and shouting as we crawled through the narrow streets. I heard one guy call out, 'Stop you idiot!' and another yelled something like, 'You're caught!' I was just hoping that he didn't mean Curtis had got caught on camera.

I remembered when I'd been doing trampolining in Gym in Year 7. I went home and tried doing a front-drop on my bed. Only there was a bit of a problem because:

1) my bed was about as bouncy as a granite springboard

2) my Robosapien (which was my best ever present from Dad, when I was twelve) was under my duvet but I didn't know.

And,

3) it turned out my bed had a terminal case of woodworm! The slats under the mattress crumbled into dust as I went into the final bounce. Just as I was about to lift my legs up ready to drop down on my front, my legs buckled under me and I collapsed sideways with Robosapien's arm gouging a lump out of my cheek. Which is cool because it means I've got this manly scar just under my left eye – like spies and really hard men have.

Of course Mum went into panic warp factor ten and jumped a red light when she was taking me to A & E; I ended up with two stitches and she ended up with an eighty pound fine. Even Mum, as calm as she is usually, nearly blew a gasket, so I just knew that the mood Curtis was in, a hefty fine was hardly going to enhance his holiday spirit.

But we trundled on through the market regardless. Flo and Vee were purring along by our side, banging and shouting and waving their arms. Finally the market stalls petered out and the road veered round to the right. Curtis pushed the car up a gear as the road straightened out. I must admit it was a relief because, as the car speeded up, at least we got a bit of a breeze to help cool us down. Driving through the market it had got so hot in the car, I felt like a joint of beef being slow roasted. But as the car picked up speed, so did Florence's gesticulating.

Belinda turned round and bit her bottom lip. 'I think perhaps you should stop, darling. Your mother looks very upset about something.'

'Well, she shouldn't ride so close, should she? We haven't time to be stopping. We're already late. We were supposed to be checking in ten minutes ago. Magenta,' he said, over his shoulder. 'I need you to be on the ball with that map to get us back on to the ring road. OK?'

Magenta gave a sigh and picked up the atlas again. 'Fine!' She flicked it open at Northern Ireland.

I was just about to give it one more go and offer

to help her when my phone bleeped with a text from Spud. It said:

Txt me wn u gt thr. Hv bg sprize 4 u. Cheers.

Magenta looked across at me and narrowed her eyes. 'Is that from Justine?'

Grrr! I couldn't help it. I know sarcasm is supposed to be the lowest form of wit, but her jealousy was really pissing me off. 'I do have other friends, you know, Magenta.'

'Oh, so Justine's your *friend* now, is she?'

I was just about to say something like, *well that's more than I can say for you* – when a bee flew in through the open window. My poor Magenta went totally bananas! She's been phobic about bees and wasps and bluebottles – in fact anything that flies and makes a buzzing sound – since she fell into a wasps' nest when she was little. Florence thought she was practising her Irish jig for the infant school country dancing display and kept telling her to keep the noise down. But in reality, she was being stung fifty-seven times by angry insects. She ended up in hospital for observation and looked as though she had measles for the next week.

So when the bee flew in, I knew how she was going to react.

'Aaaaagh!' Magenta screamed. 'Get it out! Get it out!'

'What?' Curtis yelled, turning round as he was driving – which was not a good move as he careered right across the white line and into the face of oncoming traffic – luckily nothing that was too close, but even so, a tad worrying.

Belinda grabbed the wheel. 'Curtis, I really think you should let me drive.'

'What!' he yelled again – at Belinda this time.

'Quick,' I said. I knew that this was my chance to leap to her rescue. I undid my seat belt and grabbed the road map from Magenta. 'I'll flick it out with this.'

Magenta snatched the atlas away again. 'Give it back. You've been after this ever since we set off.' She was cowering in the corner, trying to flick the bee away with the enormous book like some deranged whack-a-crock champion. I don't know what we must have looked like from behind because there was Magenta flapping like a maniac inside the car and Florence and Venice still flapping away on the outside. We must've looked like Flappers Anonymous. No wonder Wayne was honking his horn like it was on permanent loop.

'Stay still,' I said to Magenta. 'Don't aggravate it.'

'Aggravate *it*!' she snapped. 'What do you think *it*'s doing to *me*?'

'Just keep your mouth shut,' I said.

'How dare you tell me to shut my mouth!'

Durr! I love her to pieces but sometimes Magenta can be too defensive for her own good. 'I didn't mean like that – I meant so that it can't fly in your mouth and—' Uh-oh! Wrong thing to say.

'AAAAAAAAGGGGGHHHH!' she screamed even louder.

I slapped my hand over her mouth. 'Get off me,' she said, pushing my hand away. 'Let me get rid of it.'

'Please don't kill it,' said Belinda.

'Just stay calm,' I said. 'You're only making it worse.'

But the road map came down smack across my head and I keeled over on the seat again.

'Ooops! Sorry,' Magenta said. 'I thought it had landed on you.' Yeah, right!

But just then, she did the dippiest thing I've ever known her to do – EVER! She only went and opened the car door – while we were moving! 'I'm just going to let it fly out,' she explained.

'NO!' I yelled but it was too late.

I lurched across her to try and pull the door shut

but only succeeded in knocking her sideways out of the door. Luckily she was still in her seat belt, so even though her top half was dangling out over the road (still hanging on to the atlas like I was going to snatch it from her, by the way), her bum was still firmly on the seat.

I grabbed Magenta, pulling her upright and the door shut – sadly just a tad too late. As the door had opened, it had hit the front wheel of Florence's bike! And as I was hoisting her back into the car, Magenta put her arms round my neck – and let go of the road map!

Then everything seemed to happen together and in slow motion:

1) The motorbike swerved to the left, and there was a sickening grating sound from the back of Curtis's car as his bumper was ripped off. Where it had been damaged in the crash last week, it had been sticking out a bit and had got caught on one of Florence's leg chains when she'd come up alongside us – no wonder she'd been banging on the car roof for the last couple of miles.

2) The two old dears mounted the kerb and skidded to a halt in the middle of a display of fruit and veg outside a greengrocer's shop. There were

bananas and apples and enormous marrows flying everywhere. Poor Florence's bright red suit was dripping in squashed tomatoes.

3) As the road atlas left Magenta's hand, it took to the air like a giant red-and-blue-veined bat, and landed squarely on the windscreen of the four by four that Justine's family were in.

But worst of all:

4) With the atlas blocking his vision out of the windscreen, Wayne veered off the road, following in his mother's skid marks. He managed to avoid the shopfront and the two old ladies, pretty skilfully actually – I was well impressed – but ended up wrapping his brand new radiator neatly round a speed camera next to it.

Curtis slammed on the brakes and reversed back. Oh boy – you should've seen Wayne's face when he got out of the car. He stormed over to our car. 'Magenta! You stupid . . .!'

Then Magenta turned to me. 'Daniel! What did you make me do that for?'

Ggggrr! And after everything I did to help her!

So, we are *definitely* not speaking now – and that's official. Some holiday this is turning out to be.

5

Magenta

Oh my God! I think I've died and gone to hell!

Imagine your worst nightmare – multiply it by ten gazillion and you'll end up with Harry Hay's Holiday Camp. But I'm jumping ahead of myself because before we even arrived at the cesspit at the end of the world, just getting there was like a voyage through Valhalla. (Belinda's into Norse mythology – and Greek mythology, and Roman and Celtic – in fact, basically, she's a bit of a mythology anorak; but I'm cool with that because it's better than being any other sort of anorak.)

But anyway, Daniel was being a prize pain all the way here; if he wasn't sulking on his PSP, he was trying to muscle in on my job as navigator. OK, so I admit, I was a teensy bit shocked when Belinda asked me to take over as map-reader, but don't let it be said that I'm not up for a challenge. And I was doing brilliantly – most of the time! I just made one teensy little mistake when we were going through this place that was like Dumpsville, Tennessee and I missed the ring road and took us through the town centre. Dad got really peed off with me, but it wasn't my fault because:

1) The signpost had been completely sprayed over with graffiti. Although, according to Rasputin in the driving seat, I'm supposed to have developed X-ray vision and been able to see right through it. Like I'm the only one in the car with their eyes open – durr, who's doing the driving around here?

2) Gran had actually *seen* a notice about the Town Centre being closed for a French market, but did she think to lift up her visor and *tell* us to turn right? I don't think so! All she kept doing was pointing straight ahead – I might as well have been communicating with Lassie in red leathers.

And,

3) Maps are just stupid.

Then, as if getting the blame for that wasn't bad enough, Uncle Wayne's car crash got dumped on me too! I couldn't believe it! There I was, being attacked by a killer bee – excuse me for protecting myself, but some people have actually died from that plastic shock syndrome when they've been stung: I read about it in a magazine in the orthodontist's waiting room – when Daniel decided to take advantage of the situation and make a grab for the road map again. What is it with the male of the species that they seem to think that girls are useless at map-reading? It's all their Tarzan, machismo rubbish and it gets right up my nose. Which, incidentally, is exactly where the evil insect was heading, except that my quick thinking saved the day. It was simple really – all I had to do was open the door, lean out and the bee followed me to freedom. Pretty cool, eh? But then Daniel leaped on me again and I accidentally let go of the road map. And I can understand that some people might have interpreted it as my fault, but when you think about it, if:

a) Daniel hadn't jumped on me and
b) Uncle Wayne had been looking where he was going,

I'm sure the whole thing could've been very easily avoided. But, oh no, everyone blames me for everything! 'Hey, a skyscraper collapsed in China, guess Magenta must've had something to do with it.' 'Wow, there's an earthquake on the other side of the planet – uh-oh, Magenta must've been in the vicinity!' or, 'Terrible thing about that space rocket crashing into the surface of Jupiter – yep, must be Magenta again!' The problem with my family is that no one is willing to take responsibility for their own mistakes. Gggggrrr! It gets me so mad!

Anyway, it all got very unpleasant, and a lot of things were said that really shouldn't have been – like it all being my fault etc. etc. etc. But then Uncle Wayne insisted on dialling 999 so that the police had to come, and then the ambulance turned up and carted Auntie Heather off to hospital wailing about whiplash, and then a tow truck hauled the gas guzzler away for repair so, by the time we got here, it was almost midnight. Of course reception had closed, so we had to go to some creepy little side office to get our keys and didn't have the chance to have a proper look at the place until this morning.

Oh my days! You know I said the photograph on the Internet looked as though it had been recently vacated by the army? Well, scrap the *recently*. It looks as though it was vacated by the army – about fifty years ago!

Our 'chalet' – (yeah right! It's more like a dirty rabbit hutch than anything you'd see in the Swiss Alps) – was right on the edge of the campsite, about a zillion miles from any of the facilities – although from what I've seen so far, that might well be a plus.

Justine and I have to share a room with two single beds – which are so close I could practically feel her breathing on my face all last night – gross! She really needs to look at the amount of cheese and onion crisps she eats. And the 'sitting room', as the website called it, is no more than a manky bed-settee with a tiny little portable TV that doesn't even have a remote. Can you believe it? They expect you to keep getting up to change the channels like in ancient times. How downmarket is that?

Dad and Belinda's room is so small you can only just edge your way round the double bed. And the bathroom – well, what can I say? First of all, it's total misrepresentation because there isn't actually a bath in there – it's just a shower, with a toilet and a basin that are so close you bash your knees on the sink when you're sitting on the loo. But the worst thing is: they're all mouldy and smelly. Ugh! Poor Belinda took one look and nearly heaved again. Of course Justine isn't speaking to me after the journey, which is fine by me, as her conversational skills are roughly equivalent to a parrot with brain-death, but Daniel also isn't speaking to me. So that leaves me with two options:

1) befriend the gremlin, or
2) make new friends here.

I took one look at Holden over breakfast (don't even get me started on the food at this place – it makes school dinners look like haute cuisine!). He had burned baked beans all over his face and was staring at his plate of disgustingly fatty sausages and bacon.

'Waiter, waiter, there's a worm in my baked beans! Oh no, it's just my sausage.' Then he grinned this truly gross grin that was like looking into an orange and brown tumble drier. Ugh!

So that was option one out of the window: make new friends it was, then!

Dad was the only adult with us at breakfast; Belinda still wasn't feeling well, Auntie Heather had taken to her bed 'to recover' from the crash – talk about a drama queen, she only went and turned up in a surgical collar last night. Honestly! Anyone would think she'd been involved in a humungous motorway pile-up, instead of just a teensy little bump into a speed camera. And there's no consideration for the trauma that I'd been through with my bee-phobia. Anyway, she'd asked Uncle Wayne to stay with her this morning in case she took a turn for the worse (pul-ease!) and Gran and Auntie Vee had already gone down to the beach for an early-morning dip in the sea.

So I was all ready to embark on my new plan of going out and looking for new friends when the commandant (i.e. Dad) put his oar in. He lined up Daniel, Justine, Holden and me outside The Captain's Cabin as though he expected us to start singing something out of *The Sound of Music*. In case you're wondering, The Captain's Cabin is a canteen the size of an aircraft hangar with plastic shipwrecks and treasure chests all over the place and cringe-worthy signs saying things like, *The Soup Deck* and *The Food Fo'c'sle*. Ho ho ho! I must be careful I don't laugh too much – my head might drop off!

Anyway, Dad was droning on, 'I appreciate that you youngsters . . .' Why do parents use that word? They don't call themselves *oldsters*, do they? '. . . don't want to be hanging around with the adults all week . . .' Too right! '. . . but there needs to be some ground rules.' I swear he was in charge of a military junta in a former life. 'One, you do not leave the camp without permission from one of the adults and even then it needs to be for a very good reason . . .' So that was my escape plan scuppered. 'Two, you are to be back at the chalets by five o'clock so that we can all go to dinner together . . .' Oh deep joy! 'And three, you make sure Holden stays with you at all times.'

What! Not only was he expecting me to hang around with Daniel and Justine for the entire time, but he was making us take the grublet along too. That was sooooooo unfair.

'Cool,' Daniel said.

Cool? Is he mad? Having to drag the brat around with us is the most uncool thing imaginable. Justine with her freaky hair and make-up like a demented racoon is bad enough, but her brother . . . well – I'm lost for words – which just goes to show how bad the situation is. I was just about to walk back to the chalet and spend the rest of the day indoors when Daniel slipped his hand into mine.

'Can we make up?' he asked. 'I hate it when we're not speaking.'

Don't get me wrong, I was pleased that he wanted to make the peace but there was a little word that was missing – like *sorry*. 'Erm . . .' I hesitated.

Then Justine piped up. 'Get over yourself, Magenta. The hottest guy around is giving you a second chance – don't mess up again.'

'Giving *me* a second chance?' Can you believe her?

'You heard me,' she said with this smirk on her face. 'But if you don't want him, I bet there're lots of girls who do.' Then she linked arms with Daniel and pulled him off me. 'Come on, Danno, let's go and see what's happening in the pool.'

But Daniel was so sweet, he shook his arm free and came back to me. 'Hold on, Juss, I want to speak to Magenta.' He took both my hands in his and looked right into my eyes with the dreamiest look. Oooooo, I went all tingly inside. 'I'm sorry it's all got a bit out of hand, now can we please make up and get on with our holiday?'

Good enough for me – the S word was in there somewhere. 'OK,' I said, and gave him a kiss. Which would've been very romantic if a little weasel-featured cousin of mine hadn't been making snogging noises right next to us. But actually, it didn't matter because I was just pleased that we were back together again – Daniel is so mature in the way he accepts responsibility for his part. That's one of the nicest things about him.

'Hey, listen,' he said, squeezing my hand as we walked back to the chalets to change into our swimming costumes and collect our towels, 'I've got a surprise for you when we get to the pool.'

'What sort of surprise?' I asked.

'You'll have to wait and see.' He had a grin like a massive cheese spreading halfway across his face.

'Go on, tell me,' I begged. My mind was already running through the A to Z of big surprises and was picturing myself running into the pool and seeing a huge banner dangling from the flumes saying **'Daniel loves Magenta'** for everyone to see – including my cousin Justine, of course.

But, when we got to Waterworld, the indoor pool was rammed full of little kids and the queues for the flumes were humungous – and there was no sign of a banner, which was a teensy bit disappointing.

'Come on, let's try the outdoor pool,' suggested Daniel, dragging me away from the intertwined water slides and the plastic flowers that were dripping from all the pipes and girders.

'I don't want to go outside; I want to go on the Ride of Death,' squeaked Holden.

Daniel looked at me and smiled. 'Don't tempt me,' he muttered under his breath, but added aloud, so that Justine and Holden could hear, 'Maybe later, OK?' I love the way he's so funny like that.

It was incredibly hot outside, so I didn't mind going to the outdoor pool – even though it was like some relic from the nineteen fifties. There were big fountains at each end and, at the deep end, there were those diving boards that you normally only see in the Olympics. Honestly! I mean, who do they think goes on those these days?

But then came Daniel's surprise. No, not a banner

declaring his love for me, or a romantic bouquet of roses waiting at the poolside (silly me for even dreaming such dramatic gestures). Instead, standing in front of us, in a pair of way too small Speedos (gross!), was my recent ex and holder of the title Geek of the Decade – Spud!

'What!' I was in danger of causing serious self-harm, I was pinching myself so much.

'Hi, Magenta!' he grinned.

Then I turned to Daniel. 'Spud? This is your surprise?'

But Daniel was too busy greeting his mate like they'd been separated at birth.

'Hey, Spud, man!'

'Wazzup, Danno?'

Spud and Daniel did this boy thing of banging their fists together, grabbing each other's hands, then forearms, and finally bumping shoulders. Seriously – grow a life! Haven't they got anything better to do than spend time thinking up silly handshakes?

'How? Why? . . . I mean . . .' For the second time in half an hour I was finding it difficult to think of something to say.

But it didn't matter because you could hardly shut Spud up. 'Remember I told you my dad had won a Harry Hay's Holiday in a bowling competition?' Probably, but to be honest, I don't really listen when Spud's talking because if it isn't about penalty shoot-outs, it's about carburettors or tappets or some other boring boy stuff. 'So when Danno told me you were all coming here this week, I convinced Dad to take his prize at the same time. And lucky for us they weren't fully booked.'

Yep – lucky! That was just the word I'd been looking for.

Then Justine chipped in, 'You made your parents come here just so you could be with your friends – how awesome is that?'

And all the time this was going on I was trying really hard not to look at Spud's spindly little legs sticking out of his Speedos. How could I ever have gone out with him? Had I no self-respect? Although, in my defence, I seem to recall I was on a bit of a rebound thing at the time and couldn't be considered fully in control of my mind. Even so, seeing him like this with legs like pasty pipe cleaners, skin-tight swimming trunks and hair that bore a scary resemblance to a sopping wet mop, plastered all over his acne, wasn't doing much to improve his image.

'Wow, Magenta, you look amazing,' Spud

drooled. I felt a teensy little bit guilty when he said that because I hadn't been thinking very nice thoughts about him and yet he was the only one to even notice my new bikini – and that includes Daniel.

'Thank you,' I said. 'And you look . . .' Eek! Have you ever started a sentence that you know you can't finish? What was I supposed to say? Repulsive? Disgusting?

'Hi, kids!' Phew, saved by my dad. I didn't think I'd be relieved to see *him* this holiday. 'Don't mind us, we're just going to lie here and soak up a few rays before it gets too hot.'

Oh great! So now we were going to be supervised by the adults – it's one thing to issue rules and regulations but they could at least have trusted us without having to come and do surveillance. I looked over Dad's shoulder and, sure enough, there was a full battalion:

1) Belinda was in a tie-dye sarong with a straw hat that looked as though she'd not only woven it herself, but she'd gone into the fields and picked the straw by hand too!

2) Uncle Wayne was wearing cut-downs that should've been worn by a man half his age. Maybe I should suggest that he swap with

Spud – on second thoughts; Uncle Wayne in Speedos – ewwww!

3) Auntie Heather was sporting a bright green flowery one-piece costume with those foam sticky-out cups that look like rocket launchers. And, of course, no beach outfit would be complete without a neck brace – what every woman needs to look sexy by the pool!

4) And bringing up the rear were the Scissor Sisters in their very fetching, matching cozzies that looked as though they were hand-knitted at around the same time that this dump was built.

I took one look at the sorry bunch and decided that dissociation was the best policy. 'OK, so I'm just going to hang out round the other side,' I said to Daniel as I watched my embarrassment of a family set up camp on the sunbeds near the railings. 'You coming?' Before we could distance ourselves from the offending adults, Spud dive-bombed into the pool sending a tidal wave of freezing cold water over both of us. 'Eek! Spud!'

I went to grab Daniel's hand and pull him away but, can you believe it – he only went and jumped in after Spud! And then Justine and Holden followed him into the water too, shrieking like a pair of little kids. Honestly! Daniel's only just given me all that rubbish about wanting to make up with me and then he goes and abandons me again.

Hmph! I need to rethink whether or not I need a boyfriend who keeps treating me like this. Doesn't he think I have any self-respect? Well, I'll show him!

6
Magenta

So there I was, left on the side of the pool, soaking wet and all on my own. What was the point of me even having a boyfriend when he kept going off and deserting me? It was becoming very clear that Daniel didn't really care about me at all. I mean, it's a pretty mean sort of low life that goes off with his mate – and his ex (let's not forget the unfortunate incident at Dad's fortieth) – leaving his girlfriend to fend for herself on the first day of a holiday in a strange (*very* strange!) place. But I had way too much dignity to let it bother me. I wasn't going to end up like one of those pathetically needy girls who always has to have a boy around. If Belinda's taught me one thing, it's the need to be a strong individual. So I went round to the far side of the pool by myself – see if I cared!

I'd spread out my towel and was rubbing on sunscreen – (typical of Daniel – just when I needed him to rub it on my back, he was splashing around in the water like a five-year-old) – when a loud whistle blew and a voice came over the Tannoy,

'Clear the deep end. Diver on the top board. Everyone to the side.'

Wow! So people *do* still use the diving boards. I looked up and saw a boy, probably not much older than me, standing on the edge of the top board. Yeah, right! He was so bluffing. There was no way someone of my age was going to dive from *that* height; it must have been higher than a house. But then he went up on his toes, put his arms above his head and plopped off the edge – just like that! And he did this front somersault on the way down – which was amazing – although, not *quite* like the Olympics because there was a massive splash when he hit the water – but even so, I was impressed.

And, even more amazing, when he surfaced, he swam over to where I was and pulled himself out of the water – right next to me. Phwoar! Never mind a six pack – he had more like a family-sized twelve pack, with shoulders like a double-decker bus and biceps that made Popeye look like Spud. He shook his head so that the water flicked off his hair (a bit like Sirius does when he's chased the ducks into the lake in the park) and smiled.

'Hi,' he said, staring straight at me.

I looked over my shoulder to see if there was anyone else around, but there was no one within about ten metres. Whoa – I might be totally Pete Tong on this one, but I got the distinct impression he was chatting me up. Which just served Daniel right – going off and leaving me for Spud and my stupid cousin.

'Hi,' I replied, not being too friendly, you understand. After all, I hadn't decided whether or not to finish with Daniel yet, so technically, I did still have a boyfriend, but I didn't want to be rude either. 'That was really cool. How d'you learn to dive like that?'

He flopped down on the grass next to my towel and propped himself up on one elbow. Wow! Now here was someone who knew how to wear Speedos. 'I'm in a diving club. I go in for competitions and stuff.' You see – I was right! It *is* only Olympic people who use those boards! 'My name's Liam, by the way. I'm from Leeds. How 'bout yourself?'

I gave a sneaky look in the direction of the pool, just to see if Daniel was looking – but, unfortunately, he wasn't; they seemed to have found a ball from somewhere and they were all playing catch in the water. Even Dad and Uncle Wayne had joined in. Honestly, I sometimes wonder if Daniel really means what he says or if he just tells me he cares about me to keep me dangling on – well,

I wasn't going to dangle for anyone. I want a boyfriend who's a little less conversation; a little more action please. And Liam looked very much like an action man.

'I'm Magenta,' I said, turning back to Liam.

'Cool name,' he smiled. Ooooooooo, it was a very nice smile too. Actually, it's the sort of smile Daniel used to smile at me – note the use of the past tense.

'Who are you here with?' he asked. 'Parents? Friends?'

I glanced across at the menagerie over the other side: Belinda was sitting cross-legged, meditating, Auntie Heather was playing swat the wasp in robotic dance style (i.e. not moving her neck) and Gran and Auntie Vee were comparing corn plasters. Then I checked the pool where the others (adults included) seemed to have regressed to pre-school age. Nope! Nothing to associate myself with here – just wall-to-wall embarrassment.

'No, just here chilling by myself.'

'On your own?'

'I like to think of myself as a bit of an independent traveller.' I overheard Belinda telling Gran once, that before she went to Uni, she was an independent traveller – and it sounded kind of cool.

Obviously Liam thought so too. He nodded approval. 'So how old are you, Magenta?'

Uh-oh! No way could I let on that I was still only thirteen. 'Fourteen,' I blagged. But, actually, it wasn't a total lie because I am *almost* fourteen. Although Liam looked at me like he didn't believe me. You see, that's the trouble with being as honest as I am; you just can't get away with even teensy little porkies. There was nothing else for it – I was going to have to confess. 'Well, actually, it's my birthday next week.'

Liam laughed. 'So you're nearly fifteen?'

Oops! But who was I to argue? After all, I hadn't told a lie – well, not a big one like adding a whole year to my age. So it's not my fault Liam got the wrong end of the stick, is it? Anyway, I've always said I'm more mature than people give me credit for and, clearly, Liam recognised that. But I thought I'd better change the subject quickly just in case he cottoned on. 'So, how do you get the courage to go up on the top board for the first time?'

Liam laughed. 'You don't start off with the top board; you start on the lower ones and work your way up. You look like a girl with guts. Come on, I'll show you.' He stood up, took my hand and started leading me towards the diving boards.

'No really,' I protested. Uh-oh! Things were getting a bit out of hand. 'Actually, I've always thought of diving as more of a spectator sport, myself.'

Liam stopped and looked disappointed. 'Are you scared?'

'No-o!' I lied.

'So, what's the problem? I'll start you on the three-metre board – that's practically ground level.'

Yeah right – three metres sounded less like ground level and more like jumping out of my bedroom window. I looked across at Daniel – if he stood any chance of staying my boyfriend, he'd come and rescue me before I plummeted to my death.

But Daniel was completely oblivious to my plight. In fact, even worse than being oblivious to my plight, he was extremely aware of my cousin Justine's plight because she was sitting on his shoulders and he was holding on to her knees! Gggrr!

'Come on,' Liam was saying, 'you'll be fine once you get up there.'

I was trying to catch Daniel's eye all the way across the grass till we got to the ladder at the bottom of the tower of diving boards, but he didn't even look at me once. How negligent is that? There I was, being dragged towards the diving boards by a strange boy and my boyfriend didn't even notice! He was sooooo dumped!

But there was a glimmer of hope when we got to the bottom of the steps. Phew – a lifeguard was posted there ready to rescue people who were being abducted by suicidal maniacs like Liam – I was sure *he* would stop us. But he didn't! He just gave Liam the thumbs-up and asked if he wanted the pool cleared again. Help! I was getting desperate. I mean, I could hardly tell Liam I was frightened, could I? He thought I was this really cool fifteen-year-old independent traveller, and there was no way *that* person would be afraid of a teensy little springboard.

I was beginning to regret not being totally honest with him – but it was too late now; we were already heading up the steps – and talk about health and safety! They were the most rickety, slippery steps this side of Slimesville. Now, you can call me psychic, but I just knew this was not going to have a happy ending.

I was desperately trying to think of an excuse to get down (one that didn't include jumping off the board into freezing cold water and getting my hair wet) when suddenly we were on this platform and Liam was pushing me towards the springboard.

Eek! Now I knew how pirates felt when they had to walk the plank.

'Go on, then, walk out to the end and just bounce about a bit. Get a feel for the board,' he encouraged.

'After you,' I said, hoping to make a hasty exit back down the steps once he'd disappeared off the end.

'That's OK. I'll stay here to make sure you're all right,' he grinned.

'Cheers!'

Me and my big mouth. There was no way out. I had no choice but to edge my way along the diving board – feeling distinctly giddy, because it kept going boing, boing, boing under my feet. And the surface was really rough; a bit like walking along a wibbly-wobbly emery board. I couldn't even slide one foot after the other in case I ripped the skin off my feet – I had to try and walk properly, as though I did this sort of thing every day.

Of course it didn't help that every time I looked down, my knees turned to blancmange. I could see the other people in the water underneath me looking about as big as dolls. Practically ground level, my elbow! I was in danger from low-flying aircraft, I was so high. And there was what looked like a couple of footballs bobbing around just below the diving boards. But then an arm came out of the water and I realised that they were actually Gran and Auntie Vee in matching yellow swim caps doing some sort of weird stroke like synchronised swimmers from ancient times.

'Look, I'll show you.' Liam pushed past me, then stood on the end of the springboard and began bouncing up and down. Now, you might think that this was my moment to escape – wrong! He was going about a metre in the air each time and then landing back on the board (which would have looked really impressive if I'd been on the pool side; but I wasn't) and every time he landed, I practically lost my balance. I couldn't even move, let alone make my way back along the board to safety.

'Aaaagh! Stop it!' I yelled, feeling more and more queasy every time he came down and my whole body gyrated with the impact.

'Now it's your go,' he said, taking my hand and leading me right out to the end of the board.

Ohmygod! Ohmygod! Ohmygod! I was standing on the end of this humungous wobble board about a mile above the pool and struggling to keep my balance. I felt sick.

And then I decided that I didn't want to try and impress Liam any more. He might have a nice body but he did not have a very nice personality at all. So I sat down at the end of the board and folded my arms. I wasn't going to go anywhere.

And then I heard the golden words I'd been waiting for: 'Magenta! What the hell are you doing? Come down!'

It was Daniel. He'd seen me at last – phew! About time! And he was coming to rescue me – yeah!

Liam laughed, and it wasn't a nice laugh either. In fact, it was a pretty nasty chortle – the sort baddies do when you go to the pantomime at Christmas. 'Who's got an overprotective brother, then?'

'He's not my brother; he's my boyfriend,' I almost snarled. I was just about to try and get back on to my feet and start edging my way back along the board, when Liam came up behind me and started bouncing on the board again. Every time he came down, I was propelled up in the air and then smacked down on my bottom. Ouch! Not only was it scary up there, it was pretty painful too.

'Whoa! Pack it in!' I screamed.

'Why didn't you tell me you had a boyfriend?' He bounced again, only harder this time.

'OK, I'm sorry,' I confessed; maybe he had a point, but this really wasn't the best time for me to be having a discussion about my love life.

I'd already unfolded my arms and was clinging on to the edge of the board but even so, with each bounce, I was bumping nearer and nearer to the end and certain death. And the worst thing was, the end of the board was so old and worn that the sandpaper had completely disappeared and it had about as much non-slip-ability as an ice rink.

'So what else have you lied about?' he asked, bouncing down again.

'Nothing,' I said.

'So, you're still telling me you're a fifteen-year-old independent traveller?' He whacked down on the board again. Whoa! I couldn't wait for Daniel to come and save me.

'Oh, *that*!' You see, I knew I was too honest to get away with even a teensy little fib like that.

'Oi! You two!' the lifeguard shouted up – and not before time. What had he been doing while I was being tortured three metres above his head? 'Stop mucking about and come down now.'

I could see Daniel at the bottom of the steps and was just beginning to allow myself to relax a little, when it all started going belly-up – scuse the pun.

1) The dingbat lifeguard only went and blocked Daniel's way on the grounds that there were already too many people on the diving boards.

Durr – that's why he was trying to get up there, to rescue me and make one less!

2) Then Dad, Uncle Wayne and Spud spotted what was happening and all ran up too, trying to push past the lifeguard to come and save me – bless! I suppose there are some advantages to all that Tarzan, machismo after all.

3) But the dingbat lifeguard spreadeagled himself across the bottom of the ladder and wasn't budging (his biceps were like the Michelin Tyre Man, all bulging and gross) so there was no way anyone from my family could get him to move, even an inch – it would have been quite pathetic watching them try if I hadn't been holding on for dear life.

4) Then the dingbat lifeguard blew his whistle and about a dozen other Michelin Tyre Men appeared out of the undergrowth and descended on my rescuers.

5) Daniel, Dad, Uncle Wayne and Spud were all grappled to the ground and held in armlocks.

'No!' I shrieked. I tried to wave my arm to alert the lifeguards to my danger. But, oh dear what a mistake! As I let go of the board with my right hand, Liam banged down on the board again and I slithered off to the left.

'Aaaaagggghhh!' I managed to twist myself round so that I was lying across the board on my stomach but it was really digging into my tummy – there are times when a one-piece costume has advantages.

'Magenta, stay there. I'm coming to get you,' Daniel called as one of the burly guys frogmarched him away from the pool and in the general direction of the reception area.

'Anytime soon would be good!' I shouted back, slipping further and further off the edge till my whole body was dangling above the water and I was holding on by my fingertips. I didn't want to panic but I had a pretty good idea that there was no way my fingers would hold out for much longer and I was going to end up in the water, like it or not.

'That's my daughter up there,' I heard Dad's voice boom as two lifeguards dragged him away too.

And then, hallelujah, one of the lifeguards began climbing the steps. At last! What took him so long?

'Oi! Get down now,' the guy said to Liam. 'And you're banned from this pool for the rest of your stay.'

Excellent! That serves him right.

'And you too,' the man said to me. Can you

86

believe it? He was banning me from the outdoor pool just for being bullied! There's no justice in this world. 'Now give me your hand.'

But just as he reached his hand out for me to grab, I felt something go slack around my ribs. Uh-oh! My new bikini fastens with a tie at the back and another round my neck. And, unless I was very much mistaken, the one at the back had just come undone.

Oh no! I could feel my bikini top riding up. If I didn't act quickly, I was going to be left dangling, topless, with everything on show for the whole world to witness.

There was nothing else for it. It was a straightforward choice: my hair, or my modesty. And there was no contest. Instead of grabbing the guy's hand, I let go, slapped my hands across my boobs and felt myself dropping downwards.

I was just thinking that, actually, it wasn't as scary as I'd thought it was going to be, when,

'Aaagh!'

Uh-oh! I just landed on something that definitely did not feel like water – ooops!

7
Justine

You would not believe what my dork of a cousin has done now – she's only gone and got herself arrested!

Honestly, I don't know how I ever used to admire her. When we were little, right, I used to think she was really, like, awesome. I mean, even though I was three months older than her, I used to look up to her. But now I'm, like – durr – wake up and smell the mutant genome!

As if her stupid 'let's leap out of a moving car' antics on the way here weren't bad enough (poor Mum could be permanently disabled as a result), yesterday she only went and put Auntie Venice in hospital too. I mean, what sort of an idiot goes up on a diving board when she can't even dive? Like, hello! You don't need to be Mastermind to work out that the clue is in the name. Is it a sitting board? No. Is it a sunbathing board? No – it's a *diving* board!

Of course it was all because she was trying to impress some stupid boy – again. For heaven's sake, she's already going out with Danno – who is soooooo cool, by the way. Honestly, he's, like, this totally amazing guy and quite honestly, he could do so much better for himself. In fact, I don't mean to brag or anything, but it is *so* obvious that he secretly fancies me. Every time we're together, he's coming on to me – in a really subtle way, of course. But I know it must be hard for him. I mean, he lives next door to Magenta and they've got history that goes back years, so it's like he's duty bound to go out with her. And, actually, I really respect that in him – the fact that he's prepared to put what *he* wants on hold and do the decent thing by her.

Anyway, getting back to yesterday; all because of Magenta and her idiot streak, Auntie Venice now has a sprained neck and the whole of our group has been banned from the outdoor pool area – for the duration of the holiday! I was soooo mad with her.

We were sitting outside the manager's office waiting for Dad, Danno and Uncle Curtis. There'd been a bit of a scene at the pool – which was so embarrassing, and was *all* Magenta's fault – goes without saying, of course! Anyway, the security guards had taken them off and we were waiting for them to be released from custody. I had my ear pressed against the door and had just heard Dad trying to persuade the manager not to call the police.

'I am willing to give an undertaking that no one

from our party will go within ten metres of the outdoor pool again this week.'

What? No way! I was furious with him. Why should the rest of us suffer just because Mad Madge decides to flirt with some Neanderthal no-brain and then fling herself from three metres in the air to land right on top of poor Auntie Venice's head?

I could hear the manager's voice, and he sounded about as friendly as a rabid Rottweiler. He was saying, 'We have a policy of zero tolerance towards any assault on a member of our staff.'

Uncle Curtis piped up, 'No one was assaulted. My daughter was in danger and your staff were doing precious little to save her. Someone had to step up to the mark.' Sorry, Uncle – not convincing me.

The manager cut in, 'Your daughter needs to be taken in hand, Mr Orange. She is a danger to herself and others.' Too right! 'And, as a result, I now have one injured guest and two of my senior lifeguards with minor cuts and bruising – which were *not* self-inflicted!'

Minor cuts and bruising, eh? Wow, sounds like Uncle Curtis got physical. Go, Uncle! I didn't know he had it in him.

But then I heard Daniel mutter, 'Sorry. I just

needed to get up the ladder – I guess I just don't know my own strength.'

Correction – double wow! Go, Danno!

In the end the manager agreed to let them off with a warning.

When they came out Magenta was all over Daniel like bubonic plague, throwing her arms round his neck, in such a puke-fest, you'd think he'd just been let off the death sentence. 'Oh Daniel, I knew you'd come to my rescue. I can't believe you took on those lifeguards just for me. It's like in the olden days, isn't it? When knights in shining armour fought for a maiden's honour?' Vomit, vomit!

But Mum wasn't going to let them all get away with it that easily. 'For heaven's sake, all of you – brawling in public – how common can you get!'

Danno looked at me, then Magenta, and tried to stifle a grin. He said to Mum, 'I'm really sorry, Mrs Orange.' He's so buff; he knows exactly how to play people without being a total brown-noser. And he looked at me first before he looked at Magenta, which just goes to prove who he really fancies.

'And as for you, Curtis . . .'

'Not now, Heather, please,' Uncle Curtis snapped – which was obviously out of embarrassment about how his moron daughter had behaved. Then he started rubbing his hands together like nothing had happened. 'Right then, let's get back into the holiday spirit, shall we?'

'Durr – like, how?' I asked, glaring at my stupid cousin.

OK – I admit, I might have sounded a tad sarcastic, but I was really pissed off with her. Granny Florence and Auntie Venice were still at the hospital – with Belinda, of course, who'd driven them there. And Mum, Holden and I had spent three hours waiting for the guys to come out of the manager's office. So, practically the whole of our first day had been an absolute waste of time. Plus, we couldn't use the pool any more! It was so unfair. It was like we were all being punished for something that was one hundred per cent down to Magenta.

'Darling, try not to be upset with your cousin,' Mum said, smiling at Curtis. And I'm sure she only said it for his benefit. 'Accidents do happen.' Yeah, but my cousin needs to walk around with a danger sign round her neck. 'Now,' Mum went on, 'from what I remember on the Internet, there's a lovely beach we can all go down to.'

Right – like, about a mile away! This place is such a dump. Honestly, to think that last year at this time we were in Florida!

'Hey, can we go in the chairlift, like when we went skiing?' the little squirt squeaked.

Which just shows you how far it is to the beach – they have to have cable cars and special Noddy trains to get people down to the sea. It's practically a day excursion.

'Of, course, darling,' Mum replied, rubbing Holden's hair – gross! She doesn't know where he's been or what she might catch doing that.

We were all walking back towards the chairlift docking area; Danno had his arm round Magenta and was trying to keep her sweet. 'You know I'd never let anything happen to you, Magenta.' He's so patient with her.

His mate, Spud, who's a safe guy, actually – a geek, but a safe geek – was all: 'And *I'd* never let any harm come to you either.'

Now, if you ask me, *they'd* make an awesome couple: Magenta and Spud – I don't know why she ever dumped him. I mean, they are, soooo suited.

Suddenly, Mum stopped outside the campsite theatre.

'Justine, darling, look at this.' She was pointing to a poster for the Miss Hay's Holidays contest that takes place every Monday afternoon. 'Why don't you go in for it, kitten? You've got a wonderful figure now that you're filling out a bit.'

I'll be honest: it wasn't number one on my list of things to do – entering a beauty pageant. Although, on second thoughts, you never know what the prize is in these things or where they might lead. For all I know, they could even have talent scouts from all the big London agencies coming to these things.

'It'd probably mean you'd have to tone down that eye make-up of yours though, if you want to be in with a chance,' she went on.

I wasn't sure I wanted to compromise my image. 'Maybe,' I said.

'And look.' Mum was scouring the notice boards and getting worryingly into the whole holiday camp ideology. 'There's a Master Hay's Holidays competition too on Thursday – I'll speak to your father about entering Holden.'

'Holden? Do they have a category for pets?' Surely she couldn't think of entering that stick insect for a contest that was looking for the best hunk on campus.

Magenta finally prised herself away from Danno and looked at the notice board with the rest of us. 'Oh my God! I just hope Belinda doesn't see this. She'll be furious,' she gasped.

'What's that?' Uncle Curtis had been engrossed in

conversation with Dad but his ears pricked up when he heard the name, Belinda. It's so cute to see him all loved up. I was only sorry we had to miss their wedding because of stupid chickenpox.

Magenta was pointing to the same poster Mum had seen. 'They still have beauty competitions here – can you believe it? I mean, how archaic is *that*?' OK – it was decided then – if Magenta didn't approve of beauty pageants, you could definitely count me in. Then she went on, 'But look, there's a family talent contest too – on Friday.' She turned to me. 'Hey, Justine, do you remember that Cheeky Girls' routine we did at Christmas a few years back?' Uh-oh, I did not like where this was going. 'We could do that for the talent show.'

Danno laughed and slapped his fingers together. 'Oh yes, Juss – that would be wicked.' And, the awful thing is, I'm pretty sure he was being serious. 'You're always saying you want to be a singer. Now's your chance.'

'This could be your big moment,' Spud added.

'*Not* as a Cheeky Girl!' Maybe I overestimated Spud's safeness factor.

But my doofus cousin was on a roll. 'OK then, what about Christina Aguilera? We could do one of her songs.'

'There's only one of her,' I pointed out, fairly obviously.

'Yes, but we could adapt – the Aguilera Cousins.'

'Go on, Juss,' Danno encouraged. 'I'll tell you what, if you and Magenta do it, Spud and I will enter too. How's that?'

'Wicked!' Spud was seeming less safe every time he opened his mouth. 'Do you remember that street-dance jamming thing a load of us did for assembly in junior school? Sort of Run-DMC?' Surely he meant *geek*-dance? 'We could do that again.'

Danno looked a tad hesitant. 'I dunno, Spud. It was nearly four years ago and we were pretty crap then.'

'Neh! We brought the house down, man.'

'Erm . . . not sure about that, but when you tried to spin on your head you almost brought the whole stage down – backdrop, curtains, the lot.'

'Oh, I remember that – it was sooooo funny,' Magenta said. 'OK – so that's decided then. We'll all put our names down now and then we've got till Friday to rehearse. How cool is that?'

You see – that is why Spud and Magenta should be an item. They could spend their entire lives playing hunt the brain cell. Hey – I've just had a thought: how cool would it be, if I got them together again this holiday? Oh, that would be awesome! And, even better, it would leave Daniel free to go out with me – which is so obviously what he wants deep down. Wicked!

So, once Granny Florence and Auntie Venice were back from the hospital, we all trooped down to the Golden Galleon – which is basically a glorified amusement arcade with a pub next to it so the adults can keep an eye on their kids – very Las Vegas – I don't think! But the worst thing was, people were starting to stare as we walked past. Although I couldn't blame them; we must've looked like we'd just been let out from the day centre, what with Mum and Auntie Venice in their matching surgical collars. It was as though some terrible contagious condition was spreading through the family – who would be next to go down with the dreaded foam-neck disease?

Anyway, we left the adults to get on with it; Granny Florence and Auntie Venice were knocking back the Bailey's 'for medicinal purposes' and were already into the second verse of 'Sun is shining, weather is sweet', so we all decided that distance was probably the best way to save our sanity.

And I thought it was the ideal opportunity to put my matchmaking plan into action. All night I was, like: 'Hey, there's this awesome game over there where you can race motorbikes against each other. Spud, why don't you and Magenta have a go?'

Spud was so up for it, but Madge was being ridiculously clingy with Danno; 'Oooo, Daniel, will you come on it with me?' It's amazing how he puts up with it.

In the end, we all went over and rode the bikes together – except that I ended up riding pillion with Spud – and then, worse – my grub of a brother! Which was so *not* good for my image. There's still time though, so I'm not worried. But, scarily, I noticed that whichever game we happened to be playing, that freak from the diving board seemed to be lurking a few metres away, watching us. Creepy – as if he hasn't done enough damage for one holiday.

But I suppose you're wondering how Magenta managed to get herself arrested, aren't you? Well, it wasn't anything to do with the pool fiasco yesterday or the amusements last night – it happened earlier today.

We were still asleep this morning when Mum came round to our chalet in a bit of a frenzy. There was this banging on the door like someone was trying to break it down. At first, I thought there must have been another family disaster – but then I opened my eyes and saw Magenta still dribbling on to her pillow about a foot from my face – they really should do something about the closeness of these beds – so that put my mind at rest. She couldn't do anything too earth-shattering if she was asleep – could she?

I was on my way to open the door when Uncle Curtis shuffled out of his and Belinda's bedroom in his pyjamas. He rubbed his eyes and peered out of the door. But when he saw Mum, he really didn't sound too happy.

'Oh, morning, Heather. What time is it?' he grunted.

'Time you were up. We've been awake for hours.' Mum almost mowed him down in her rush to get to me. 'Now, Justine, darling – come along. No time to lose. We need to get you ready for your big day. I've managed to get you an appointment at the hairdresser at nine o'clock so you need to come and have breakfast now, before the rush.'

Whoa! Since my decision yesterday to go in for the Miss Hay's Holidays, I'd been having second thoughts. I mean, as appealing as the idea was of going in for it just as a way of getting back at

Magenta, I needed to ask myself, was a beauty contest really the way forward for me? As much as I didn't want to sing a duet with Madge the Moron, I thought the talent contest was more likely to get me noticed for my singing, whereas the beauty contest would only be judging me on my looks. Although Mum's right – I *do* have a nice figure. I mean, you should've seen Danno and Spud in the pool yesterday (before we were so unfairly banned); they couldn't keep their eyes off me.

'Aw, Mum! Do I have to?'

Then Magenta poked her head out of the blanket. 'Wow, Juss – are you having your hair done like Christina Aguilera for our act? What are you having, extensions? I was going to go into town and try and get hold of a wig, but extensions sound wicked.'

'Durr! No.' I couldn't believe she thought I'd go to all the expense of having extensions just to do some stupid duet with her – and I hadn't even said I was doing the Christina thing anyway. I was thinking I might do a solo, then I could really show off my talent.

Mum waited in the sitting room while I started to get dressed. Suddenly, Magenta sat up. Her eyes narrowed. 'You're not!'

'What?'

'You're not going in for that beauty contest?'

I shrugged. 'Haven't made my mind up yet.'

'How could you?'

I leaned over and looked her right in the eye. 'Listen, Little Miss Mayhem, you breathe one word of this to that stepmother of yours and you're dead meat. Understood?' The last thing I needed was a first-class guilt trip and all Belinda's feminist stuff rammed down my throat. I mean, don't get me wrong, I think Belinda's cool and it's brilliant that Uncle Curtis has found someone else after all this time – but sometimes, she's so far over the top, she's halfway down the other side.

'Just wait till I tell Uncle Wayne that you've threatened me,' she said.

'Ooooo, quaking in my flip-flops.'

Magenta was sitting up with her arms folded, trying to look hard. 'If you go in for this, Justine, I refuse to go in for the talent contest with you.'

'Fine by me.' I picked up my bag and headed for the door.

'Come along, darling!' Mum called.

'Coming,' I replied. As I was leaving the bedroom, I turned back and said to Magenta, 'Not a word – OK?'

By the afternoon, Mum had had my hair done in

a sort of tousled style that wasn't quite as Goth as I usually like but was a sort of compromise. I can understand that these competitions are quite mainstream, so if I want to win the heats today and go through to the regional finals, I'll need to toe the line. Mum had also bought me a new dress and a new bikini especially for the contest so I was starting to warm to the idea after all.

As we approached the theatre, we could see quite a crowd gathered outside.

'Wow, look how many people are queuing,' I said to Mum. 'Do you think they're all contestants?' I was blown away. I hadn't realised how popular these things are or how much competition there'd be.

'No, darling, I expect most of them are spectators.'

Spectators! Jeez! I hadn't realised that people would come to watch me. I was starting to feel a bit nervous.

But, the closer we got, the more I realised that some of the women weren't actually queuing, they seemed to be shouting about something. They were sitting on the ground right in front of the theatre, blocking the door and holding placards above their heads that said things like: *CALL OFF THE CATTLE*

MARKET and *MORE THAN JUST PRETTY FACES.*
I couldn't believe it – they were objecting to the Miss
Hay's Holidays competition. These people couldn't
be serious. Surely they could see that the pageant
was just a bit of fun? But then I saw them; there,
right at the front, was Belinda – and who should be
her sidekick? My clown of a cousin!

'Magenta!' I yelled at her. 'What the hell do you
think you're doing?'

'We want respect! We want respect!' she
chanted, completely ignoring me. She had this big
piece of cardboard in her hands that read: *BAN
THE BIMBOS.* Can you believe it – bimbos! Just
wait till I get hold of the selfish cow. She knew I
wanted to win this and she deliberately set out to
ruin it for me.

Then the security guards who'd hauled Dad and
Uncle Curtis away yesterday rolled up with
loudhailers. They were saying things like, 'Come
along now, ladies . . .'

But Belinda shouted above the others, 'Women!
Don't patronise us – we are *women* – not ladies.'

And Magenta kicked off again, 'We are women;
we want respect! We are women; we want respect!'
Who did she think she was kidding? But then all the
others joined in too!

Mum and I looked at each other.

'Of course, I blame your Grandmother Florence,' Mum said. '*My* mother would never allow such common behaviour.' She gave me a little kiss on the cheek. 'I'm so glad you take after my side, darling.'

And then it happened. There was a wailing of sirens as a swarm of police cars, all with blue flashing lights, descended on the scene.

The police officers marched into the middle of the group. 'Break it up now, ladies.'

'WOMEN!' Magenta bellowed at one of them.

Uh-oh! So *not* the way to speak to an officer of the law! The next thing we knew, four policemen had grabbed hold of her, one on each arm and leg, and hauled her off into the back of a police car. Most of the protesters tossed their placards on to the ground and dispersed the minute they saw Magenta get arrested. But Belinda leaped to her feet and started bashing one of the police officers with her sheet of cardboard, screaming, 'She's a minor! Leave her alone!'

Then they grabbed her and hauled her into the van, too.

Awesome! I couldn't wait to tell Danno.

8
Daniel

Wow – I am so proud of Magenta. One of the things I love most about her is the way she isn't afraid to stand up for her principles – and you should have seen her yesterday! Talk about Suffragette City!

The guys had gone off for a game of footie and the women were doing their own thing. Curtis and I were nine goals up – Wayne had put the gnat-bite in goal and, even with Spud on his side (who's been training like mad to get into the squad at school next season), it was like Playschool versus Man U – no chance! I know it probably wasn't very nice of me, but I'd had three days (and four nights!) of the termite's terminally crap jokes, so I thought I'd give him a taste of his own medicine.

'Hey, Holden, I hear you're changing your name to Cinderella,' I whispered in his ear when we broke for half-time.

'Huh? What are you on about?' the sluglet said.

'Well, you're always running away from the ball!' Which I thought was moderately amusing.

Unfortunately for me, the nerd only burst into tears then ran and told his dad that I'd been horrible to him!

'Daniel, can I have a word, please?' Wayne was looking none too pleased.

Uh-oh, I should have known never to under-estimate the power of the grub-meister. But before Wayne could say anything, this weird Justine-look-a-like type android, with hardly any make-up and wearing an ordinary dress, came running on to the pitch.

'Juss?' I wasn't even sure it was her, she looked so normal.

'Hey, Danno, you'll never guess . . .' She was really excited. 'Magenta's only gone and got arrested.'

'What?'

Curtis nearly choked on his water bottle. 'What? How? Where's Belinda?'

Justine flapped her hand. 'Oh, she's been arrested too.'

'What!' Curtis and I both said together. And we were off the pitch and into the car faster than you can say Batman and Robin.

By the time we got to the police station, Belinda had been released on police bail for assaulting a police officer but Magenta was still being held, 'awaiting a social worker' because she was under-age.

'Never mind the social worker, I'm her father!' Curtis yelled at the desk clerk. For a minute I thought he was going to be arrested too; but luckily he wasn't. So Belinda and I hung around waiting for them, and about an hour later they both came out looking majorly relieved.

'Yay! I've been let off with a caution,' Magenta grinned. Then her face crumpled and she bit her lip in that really cute way she has. 'I'll understand if you're ashamed of going out with me because I have a criminal record.'

I gave her a big kiss. 'Ashamed? No way – my girlfriend's a real-life political campaigner!'

She snuggled up to me and I felt really strong and protective. 'I am, aren't I? I'm helping to emaciate women.'

'I think you mean *eman*cipate.' She's so sweet the way she muddles her words.

'Whatever! Either way, I'm changing the world.' She looked up at me with those gorgeous eyes of hers. 'And in a good way, too!'

Of course, it wasn't quite such good news for Belinda because she had to appear at the Magistrate's Court in town this afternoon. What with Curtis and me being hauled off by security on

Sunday and Magenta and Belinda getting arrested yesterday, there was a bit of a theme beginning to emerge on this holiday. In fact, the manager has written Curtis a formal warning, saying that if any one of our party steps out of line again, we'll all be evicted immediately. I just hope we can last out till after tomorrow when it's Florence's seventieth birthday. That was the reason for the holiday in the first place, so it would be nice to think that we'd stayed the distance – for her sake, if nothing else.

While Curtis and Belinda went to court, Florence and Venice went off to play bingo and Heather took Wayne into town to show him a dress she'd seen when she'd been shopping with Justine. So, this afternoon, the junior branch of the Orange party had actually been allowed some adult-free time to ourselves. Of course the downside of that was that we had to take Horrid Holden with us; Juss's mum had given us all strict instructions not to let him out of our sight.

So we went down to the sea and the good thing was, not only was there miles and miles of sand, but there was also a healthy variety of water sports taking place. Justine and Spud were eyeing up the huge rubber bananas that were being dragged behind motorboats, while I was fascinated by the speedboat that was pulling a parasail behind it the length of the beach.

Holden was boring us into brain-death with his joke repertoire; this time inspired by the herd of flea-ridden donkeys that were giving little kids rides along the sand.

'What do you call a donkey in outer space?'

'I don't know; what do you call a donkey in outer space?' I thought I'd better humour him after the incident at the footie yesterday.

'Lost!' he grinned.

'Brilliant,' I said, with a certain lack of conviction.

'Shut it, flea-features!' Juss snapped. Then she turned to me. 'So, Danno, you fancy a flight in a parachute?'

I put my hands in the *back-off* position. 'No way! Just admiring the boat – that's all.' Call me Mr Boring, but I'd seen enough action for one holiday; I just wanted to chill in the sun with my beautiful girl by my side.

'How about you, Magenta?' Spud suggested. 'You wanna go on the banana with me?'

Magenta gave him a look that could have fried an egg in ten seconds. 'If I'm going to die young, I can think of a squillion better ways to do it than being battered to death by a ginormous piece of rubber fruit, thank you, Spud.'

'Parasailing then?' Spud might be my best mate but he's never been one to fully grasp the 'no' concept.

Except that, I've known Magenta for over ten years and, normally, I'd have put money on the fact that she'd rather have poked herself in the eye with half a rainforest of sharp sticks than be dangled by a strap a few hundred metres above the North Sea. But not today! Of course, it was all to do with this ridiculous vendetta that's going on between her and Juss. The minute the words had left Spud's lips, Justine was in there.

'Yeah, right! My cowardy-custard cousin, going parasailing? Get real. She couldn't even hack it three metres above a swimming pool, never mind three *hundred* metres above open water.'

Magenta's eyes narrowed. Oh no! I'd seen that look before.

'Actually, Justine,' she said, 'my experience on the diving boards has given me an appetite for excitement. So, cheers, Spud – I might take you up on that offer.'

Had she taken leave of her senses? 'Really?' I queried.

'Of course, really!' Her face tightened into a

scowl. 'You don't think I've got the nerve either, do you? Oh my God! My own boyfriend thinks I'm gutless!'

Why do girls do that; twist things round to make you out to be the bad guy while they look hard done by? 'I never said that!' I protested.

Then Spud put his oar in again. 'I don't think you're gutless, Magenta.' Cheers, Spud! Way to go – supporting your mate.

'Thank you, Spud!' Magenta folded her arms in that way that she does when she's set her mind on something and a whole herd of rampaging rhinoceroses with shopping vouchers for a year won't make her change her mind. 'Come on, Spud. We'll show them who's gutless.' She walked to the back of the queue, dragging Spud with her.

I have enough sibling rivalry when I'm at home with my iguana-featured brother; the last thing I wanted was the cousinly version when I was on holiday. I was getting sick of it.

'You don't have to do this, you know, Magenta.' I ran after them.

'I know.' Her voice was clipped.

'It doesn't make you any less of a person if you back down.'

Eeek! Wrong thing to say. 'I *know*!' Now her voice

was so clipped, it was almost stripped down to bare metal.

I tried a different approach. 'I'll still love you, even if your feet never leave the ground as long as you live.'

Her eyes flickered sideways momentarily. 'Hmph!'

OK – I'd played my '*love*' ace and she still wasn't budging. I was fresh out of ideas for talking her out of this suicide mission – and then Holden wormed his way under Justine's arm and poked his nose in. 'What about me?' he asked.

'What about you?' Justine snarled at him.

'Can I go on the parachute?'

She paused for a moment. 'Don't tempt me.'

But Holden's a bit like woodworm – once it takes hold, it's difficult to get rid of. 'Mum made you promise to look after me,' he persisted. 'And you're not. I'll tell Dad.'

'Aw! Diddums!' Justine mocked. Then she winked at me. 'I know, while Magenta and Spud are waiting, why don't we play hide and seek in the sand dunes? You go hide, while Danno and I count to . . . umm, let's see . . . a million, and then we'll come looking for you.'

He gave her this *yeah-right* look. 'You can't even count to a million.'

'Oh yeah? Try me,' Justine said. 'One, two, three . . . better get hiding.' And Holden was off. 'That's got rid of him for the afternoon. So, Danno, why don't we go for an ice cream while the Death Wish Duo are waiting? We'll be back by the time it's their turn.'

I really didn't want to leave Magenta. I knew she was mad with me for trying to talk her out of this latest lunatic idea of hers, but I still wanted to be there to support her. Although, Justine was right, there were still three people ahead of them in the queue, so we'd got time to get there and back, no probs.

'Do you want anything?' I asked her.

'I'll be fine.' Her voice wasn't sounding any more forgiving.

Spud put his arm round her shoulder. 'No worries, mate. You go get your ice cream. I'll look after her.'

Gggrrr! No worries? It was stuff like that that made me think, yes, worries!

'Come on, Danno,' Justine said, grabbing my arm and hauling me off in the direction of the kiosk by the chairlift.

'We won't be long,' I reassured Magenta.

'Whatever!' Only this time her expression looked

like she wanted to fry *me* in ten seconds, never mind an egg!

Have you ever done anything that, when you look back, you know it's been for the best, but you really wish you hadn't done it? It's like you've been all warm and cosy and trusting in something (or some*one*, in my case) and then – BOSH! Reality hits and the whole security blanket of your belief system shatters into a thousand tiny pieces and you're left out in the freezing cold. You want, more than anything, to turn back the clock and snuggle up, all warm and cosy again, but now you know the truth and that the cosiness wasn't real – it was just some fantasy – an illusion. Well, that's what happened to me at the ice cream kiosk.

My mum has a saying; she says, 'Once your eyes are open to the truth, there's no shutting them again.' And in the space of a few minutes at the kiosk, the warm cosy duvet of my relationship was harshly pulled back to reveal the horrible and previously unimaginable truth: Magenta, the most wonderful, beautiful girlfriend in the world (or so I thought); the girl of my dreams (nightmares, more like); the one I wanted to share my life with for ever (rewind, think again!) was nothing more than a cheap, two-timing player – TWICE OVER!

The first sign that my world was about to come crashing round my ears was as Juss and I were walking towards the ice cream hut.

'I think you're amazingly trusting, you know, Danno,' she said.

There was something about the way she said *trusting* that got me started on what Mum calls, The Worry Train. It was like a tiny little weevil, boring its way into my thoughts – on turbo drive. 'What d'you mean?'

She shrugged. 'Oh, it's probably nothing.' We'd got to the hut and she was studying the laminated poster of ice creams like it was an introduction to Quantum Physics.

'Come on, Juss – it must be something or you'd have kept quiet. What's going on?'

'Well,' she sighed, like she was tussling with some huge dilemma. 'I didn't want to say anything, but haven't you noticed how close Magenta and Spud have been this holiday?'

I looked back to the edge of the beach at Magenta, but got the shock of my life. Magenta was already being strapped into a life-jacket by the two blokes who were organising the parasailing.

'Quick!' I said to Juss. 'It's already her turn. We have to get back.'

'Oh yes,' Justine said calmly. 'I heard that kid in front of her telling her mum and dad that she'd changed her mind. Still, you can still watch her from here, can't you? And it looks like Spud's got everything under control.'

And then I saw what she meant. Spud was standing in front of Magenta and seemed to be fastening something across her chest – and, although it was hard to tell from a distance, it looked like he was grinning. Magenta was shaking her hands in the air, like she does when she's panicking, and I saw Spud put his arms round her. I felt a knot tighten in my chest and my jaw went tense. That should be her boyfriend's job, helping her into the harness and then calming her down; *my* job – not Spud's.

'They're just mates,' I argued – and even I thought it sounded feeble. 'That's all – friends. But look, I really should get back there to watch her.'

'Sure,' Juss said, ordering herself a three-scoop ninety-nine. 'As long as you're cool with it, forget everything I said. Who am I to interfere? Do you want a triple scoop too?'

'Erm . . .' Cool with what? There was nothing to be cool with, was there? My eyes were still firmly fixed on Magenta and Spud. The two guys were holding open the massive red and white sail and I could hear the engine of the speedboat as it hit the throttle and pulled away. I saw her leaning back now and, the further the boat went out to sea, the more the rope that was attached to her parachute was tightening. My heart, which had jumped right out of my chest and into my mouth, was beating faster than the wickedest drum and bass remix you'd ever heard. I saw Magenta take one step, two and then she was off. Up in the air she went. Oh, she looked so fabulous, like she was sitting on a swing in the sky. I hoped she was going to be OK – I realised my teeth were clenched together so hard I'm surprised I hadn't caused serious root-canal damage. And I'd stopped breathing too. Then I saw her waving. Relief! She must be all right. I relaxed a bit and waved back. Wow – she was so brave. I loved her so much in that second – freedom fighting, parasailing – was there no end to the talents of my true-love? And that's when it hit me: she wasn't waving at me – she was waving at the ground where she'd taken off – at Spud! Justine was right – there was something going on between them! Only I'd been too blind to notice.

'Here you go.' Justine handed me an enormous ice cream.

But I was rooted to the spot. I couldn't move. My

feet had sunk into the sand and I was completely paralysed with the shock.

'Danno?' Juss elbowed me. 'Here, take it, it's already starting to drip down the side.'

And then, a double whammy! A figure slimed his way out from round the back of the kiosk and leaned, casually, against one of the raffia beach umbrellas with a smirk on his face.

'Hey, aren't you supposed to be with that Magenta chick?' It was that letch, Liam from Leeds – the kid from the diving boards. His baseball cap was on sideways with the peak over one ear and, even though it was about ninety degrees, he was wearing a hoody and low-riders.

'What's it to you?' I asked, suddenly shaken out of my state of shock. 'Cheers, Juss.' I took the ice cream from Justine.

He grinned and raised one eyebrow (actually, I've always wanted to be able to do that – you know, like Roger Moore does when he's 007 in the James Bond films?).

'Nut'in'.' He was trying to sound like some sort of bad boy gansta.

'So piss off then,' I said, trying to sound harder than I actually felt.

But he stood his ground. 'Not the kinda honey

you could ever really trust though, is she? If you get my meaning.'

There it was – the T word again, wheedling its way into my brain. 'Why don't you just crawl back into whatever hole you came out of.' I tried bogging him out, but a grain of sand blew in my eye and I had to blink it away.

Liam straightened up, turned his cap round so that the peak was at the back, and said, very quietly, 'Only she's very liberal with her lips, your *girlfriend*.' Then he raised his eyebrow again. 'You get me?'

Oh, I got him all right! I could feel the ice cream running down my hand but I didn't care. I didn't want it any more. Right now, I just wanted to ram the whole three scoops (with flake) right in the face of stupid Liam from stupid Leeds in his stupid hoody. Actually, the only time I've been to Leeds was when Dad took Joe and me to watch the Leeds Rhinos play rugby and it was a pretty cool place – which makes it even more surprising that it spawned someone like that jerk.

He gave a sneer then turned and bowled away. I was just about to run after him and rugby tackle him in the sand dunes when Justine caught my arm and my ice cream flipped backwards right down my chest, right down my best swim shorts and into the sand.

'Justine!' I yelled at her. Not that I wanted to eat it, but she'd just destroyed my weapon of choice against the demon diver.

But she ignored me. She was laughing and pointing towards the edge of the beach where the queue was for the parasailing. 'Oh my God! The Queen of Calamity strikes again!'

I'd been so distracted by Justine and Liam the Liar (he *was* lying – wasn't he?) that I'd forgotten to watch Magenta and she was coming in to land already – although not very well from the looks of it.

People were running in every direction. The two ground assistants were sprinting along the beach (well, trundling really – they were too big to sprint), shouting up at the parachute. Then I heard, 'AAAAAGGGGGH!'

Magenta was hanging from the straps of the parasail, screaming at the top of her voice and careering wildly towards the beach. She overshot the two guys, legs flailing madly; overshot the rest of the queue who scattered and dived for cover – some face down in the sand, others into the sea – and was heading straight for Kiddies' Corner.

'Quick!' I shouted to Justine. 'We've got to help her.'

As the massive canopy wafted above her head,

the herd of donkeys that had been plodding sedately up and down took fright and began stampeding across the beach towards the sand dunes. Little kids were screaming, parents were panicking, but Justine seemed totally unfazed.

'Ooooh! Too late,' she said, licking her ice cream as cool as anything. 'Looks like Spud's already on to it. Shame.'

And she was right. Spud had overtaken the two assistants (he must have been training seriously hard to get into the footie squad – either that or the guys were even more unfit than they looked) and was leaping in the air trying to catch hold of Magenta's foot before she smashed into the helter-skelter.

'Still,' Justine went on, 'look on it as a lucky escape. I mean, do you honestly want to go out with someone who's "liberal with her lips"? You're worth more than that, Danno. Come on; let me buy you a Coke. The other two can bring the bags and stuff – if they can prise themselves away from each other, that is.'

I watched Spud take hold of Magenta's foot. The two ground assistants caught up with him and guided her gently to the ground, then she turned and flung her arms round Spud as the parasail floated down behind her.

A lump the size of a basketball formed in my throat.

Magenta was jumping up and down, the way she does when she's excited. Now Spud was helping her out of the chute and they were laughing.

My eyes felt as though someone had rubbed onions in them. I blinked wide – I didn't want Juss seeing me upset.

If Magenta was being *that* friendly with her ex (and let's face it, even though he's my mate, I could hardly call him a looker), who's to say she hadn't been as liberal with her lips as Liam claimed? The harsh reality was staring me in the face. Maybe Liam was right. Maybe Justine was right. Maybe I was the world's biggest idiot!

'I need some space,' I told Justine.

'Hey, Danno!'

But I ignored her.

I'd been a prize prat, and everyone could see it but me. I headed along the beach in the opposite direction from the water sports, away from the holiday camp, away from everything.

And I just kept on walking.

9
Magenta

Oh my God! Didn't I tell you this was the worst holiday ever? And this afternoon it just got a gazillion times worse.

Wait for it – Daniel has only gone and escaped! But, even worse, he didn't take me with him. For some reason that is totally beyond my understanding, he took the evil elf – Holden! Auntie Heather reckons he's kidnapped him, but personally, I don't think Daniel's that masochistic. In fact, if anything, I should think it's Holden who's abducted Daniel.

It all started when we were on the beach. Justine, who, I've decided, is possibly even more evil than her brother, was taunting me so much about my terrible experience on the diving boards (and even appears to have brainwashed Daniel into her way of thinking) that I was forced to try and prove my courage to both of them by going parasailing. And, oh boy, did I regret it. But, if there's one thing I learned from Belinda, it's the importance of owning your own mistakes. And, believe me, parasailing was certainly one BIG mistake – on many levels.

1) It is *not* the easiest and least life-threatening of all water sports as advertised on the billboard next to where we lined up. It is very, very dangerous and threatened not only my life but also the lives of anyone on the beach who was within a hundred metres of the landing area.

2) The stupid sail had a mind of its own and decided to do a one-eighty turn in mid-air. Like – hello! Person attached!

3) The two gorillas who were on the beach strapping people into and out of it were all, 'We told you not to pull on the risers.' Like it was *my* fault. I'm thinking, if you don't want people pulling the risers, don't put them there. It's hardly brain surgery, is it? I mean, what else are you supposed to pull on when you want to stop? It's not like there's a brake or anything.

4) Plus, they seemed to have been taking a break from personal hygiene which, when they have to get all up close and personal putting the life-jacket on and stuff, is sooo gross. In fact, I think they should be reported for causing a nasal assault.

And, much as I hate to admit that my cousin might be even a teensy little bit right on anything,

5) This sort of thing should only be allowed in homes for the insane or those with a death wish.

Mind you, you would have thought that as a loyal and loving boyfriend, Daniel would at least have had a go at Justine when she was goading me into it, but, oh no! He only went and sided with her – and then deserted me in my hour of extreme trauma to go and get an ice cream. See what I mean about her brainwashing him?

Honestly! I would be furious with him – only he's not here to be furious with. And I must admit, I am starting to get a teensy bit worried about him. None of us took our phones to the beach, so as soon as I got back to the chalet I tried ringing him – but Uncle Wayne picked up! So he obviously hadn't been back to the chalet to collect his. It's been four hours now and it's starting to get dark. Even the police are involved.

'My baby!' Auntie Heather was wailing as Uncle Wayne showed the woman police officer a photo of Holden on his digital camera. 'Why aren't you out there searching for my little boy?' she snapped. 'That idiot could have taken him anywhere in this time.' Then she glared at me. 'I told Curtis this trip should only be for family.'

Humph! Daniel *is* family – well, practically. He's

lived next door to Gran all his life, so, if you think about it, he's known Gran longer than either me or Justine – which is a bit weird actually.

The WPC tried to calm her down. 'Now, Mrs Orange, we don't know for certain that Daniel Davis has abducted your son.'

Auntie Heather was off again, 'Waaaaaaagh!'

Uncle Wayne, the voice of reason, stepped in. 'Justine, love, try to remember the exact details of last time you saw Holden. Where was he going? What was he doing?'

'I've told you.' She sounded a tad tetchy to me, but then I suspect that was her guilty conscience. 'Daniel and I were playing hide and seek with him.' Yeah, right! *You hide and we'll seek you in a couple of hours,* more like. 'He went to hide in the sand dunes, but before we had time to go looking for him, Magenta crash-landed her parachute into the herd of donkeys and all hell was let loose.' Everyone turned to look at me. Whoa! So many evil glares – I'm surprised I didn't turn to stone on the spot. Honestly, talk about dumping the blame! 'And then, of course, after Magenta stopped getting all the attention . . .' Again, so many horrible looks! '. . . Daniel had disappeared and Holden was nowhere to be found.' She dabbed a (fake) tear from the corner of her eye. 'We looked everywhere, Dad, really we did.'

Well, we all know what career my cousin's destined for, don't we? And the Oscar for the most conniving little cow on the face of the Earth goes to . . .

'Well, the sand dunes stretch for several miles along the coast, so it would've been very easy for him to have got lost.' I think the policewoman was trying to reassure everyone. 'We've got officers with dogs out searching for him and a helicopter with heat-seeking equipment . . .'

But it wasn't quite working.

'WAAAAAAGGGGGH!' Auntie Heather was on full panic mode – not that I could blame her. Although, I wasn't too worried myself because:

1) I know Daniel, and if he was with Holden, he'd be taking care of the little nerd probably better than his own sister would. Daniel's so sweet, he loves all living creatures, and I know sometimes it's easy to think that Holden doesn't count, but in general he does fulfil most of the criteria.

2) I also know Holden, and even if he's not with Daniel, his powers of survival are scarily good. Believe me, Justine's tried many times to get rid of him, but he just keeps bouncing back.

Just as Auntie Heather was building to a crescendo, Dad poked his head round the door. We were squashed into Uncle Wayne's chalet; Uncle Wayne, Auntie Heather, Justine, me and two police officers. And believe me, it was anything but cosy!

'Any news?' Dad asked.

We all shook our heads.

He came in and stood next to me. It was about time I had some moral support.

'Mum and Venice have gone into town on the bike,' he said to his brother. 'Just in case they've wandered right along the coast.'

We all nodded. The police officers were whispering in a corner and the atmosphere was Serious Arctic!

'How's Belinda?' Uncle Wayne asked to try and break the tension.

Dad shrugged. 'Got a migraine. She's gone to bed.'

We all nodded again. Belinda had been bound over to keep the peace this afternoon at her court hearing, but we'd agreed that it was probably best not to mention the fact in front of the police.

The male police officer sat down again. 'Has anyone tried to contact Daniel Davis's family?'

Oops! I'd picked up Daniel's phone from his

bedside table (it was really cute, he'd got a pic of the two of us kissing on his screen – sweet!) but it hadn't occurred to me to try and contact Mary. I scrolled down the numbers till I came to one that said *MUM MOB*. But it went straight on to voicemail.

'Try Trevor,' my dad suggested. Trevor is Daniel's dad. 'I'm sure I heard Mary tell Belinda that there wasn't any reception in Scotland.'

But the spooky thing was, I was just scrolling back up again to the Ds, when my dad's phone rang.

'It's Mum,' he said, looking at the caller ID. But then he flipped open his phone and said, 'Daniel? What on Earth . . .?' Everyone went quiet. You could've heard one of Auntie Heather's foam curlers drop on to the carpet – which is probably not a very good metaphor because the carpet was practically worn down to the concrete floor it was so threadbare and Auntie Heather's foam curlers have metal bits inside – but anyway, I'm sure you get the picture – it was *really* quiet. We were all straining to try and hear. 'Uhuh . . . uhuh . . . uhuh . . .'

'Dad!' I whispered, exasperated. 'What's with the uhuh? Just put him on speaker.'

But Dad flapped his hand at me in a *shut up* sort of way. 'Uhuh . . . uhuh . . . uhuh . . .' Oh my days!

This was soooooo frustrating. 'Uhuh . . . uhuh . . . OK, I'll see you in about ten minutes.'

I held my hand out. 'Let me speak to him.' But Dad flipped shut his phone and shook his head. 'I'm sorry, but he doesn't want to talk to you, love.'

What! Can you believe it? My boyfriend disappears off the face of the Earth for four hours and then he doesn't even want to talk to me! He is soooooo dead meat when I get hold of him.

Then Dad gave us a quick rundown of what Daniel had said. 'Apparently, Daniel had been upset about something that had happened on the beach . . .' Oh great, all eyes on me again! '. . . so he'd gone for a stroll on his own and ended up walking all the way down to the pier in town. He hasn't seen Holden since Justine sent him off to play in the sand dunes . . .' Yes! People were starting to give Justine the demon look now – about time. Belinda always says, the truth will out. Well, it's out now, isn't it, Ms Nelly-Nasty-Knickers! 'Mum and Venice found him near the pier. I'm just going to pick him up in the car,' Dad went on. 'He's still in his swimming shorts apparently and frozen, so I'll need some of his clothes. Magenta, if you could sort something out, please?'

I grabbed the nearest T-shirt, jeans and trainers

from Daniel's bedroom. 'I'll come with you.' I didn't know if I wanted to hug him or murder him, but right now, just seeing Daniel again would be soooo lovely and I'd decide what I wanted to do later.

'Er . . .' Dad looked uncomfortable. 'Actually, he doesn't want to see you at the moment, love.' Then he gave me the pitying look that he usually reserved for the terminally ill or the bag lady who sits on the steps outside M&S. 'Give him some time, OK? I don't know what happened, but Daniel's very hurt.'

'Nothing happened!' I protested, glaring at my cousin. Ggggrrrr! Call me Mystic Madge, but I just knew she was behind all this.

Justine wiped another fake tear and sobbed, 'My brother's missing and all you can think about is your love life.'

Which set off Auntie Heather again. 'Waaaaagggh!'

Oh great! Whether Daniel wanted to see me or not, I was outta here. Dad was heading down the row of chalets towards ours, so I ran after him.

'Please, Dad. Nothing happened. This is all Justine's fault.'

'I'm getting a little sick of hearing you blame Justine for everything, Magenta.' *Me* blame *her*? That's rich! 'Your relationship problems are no one else's fault but your own.' Oh yeah? Shows how much he knows about relationships. 'So, Daniel has asked me to go and pick him up on my own, and that's what I'm going to do.' When we got to our chalet, he put his fingers to his lips. 'Sssh, Belinda's asleep. I don't want you waking her. I've only come for the car keys, now you go back to Uncle Wayne's with the others.'

If he thought I was going to go back to that nest of nastiness, he could think again. 'I'd rather stay here.' I went to turn on the TV but Dad waved his hand in a no-way gesture. 'What – no TV?' I hissed.

'I don't want you waking up Belinda. If you're going to stay here, you can stay in your room and read.' Then he picked up his car keys and left.

Read! I'd finished all my magazines ages ago. I knew Justine had a couple stashed under her bed, although I must admit, *Kerrang!* wasn't my usual bedtime reading. Still, it was preferable to going back to the Hammer House of Horrors. I tiptoed across the sitting room and turned the door handle to the bedroom I shared with my cousin.

But as soon as the door opened this evil odour hit me – like mucking-out time at the zoo. Ewww! It smelled like something had died in there – about a month ago. Yuk! This was worse than when Sirius has rolled in something nasty in the woods. And I thought the parasailing guys had personal hygiene issues! My cousin really needs to take a serious look at her attitude to cleanliness. I put my hand over my nose and groped the wall to flick on the light switch, but I'd forgotten, the bulb had gone this morning.

And then I heard it!

It was a strange sound – a gruff, snuffling, panting, wheezing sort of sound, like an asthmatic elephant. And it was coming from the direction of *my* bed. Whoa! This was freaking me out. There was something unmentionable in there and, in a split second, I narrowed it down to three possibilities:

1) an elephant with asthma really had stumbled into my room to die,
2) a homeless person had decided to take refuge in there, or
3) our chalet had a ghost!

Working on the Laws of Probability (I'm not totally sure what the Laws of Probability are, but Dad's always using them to try and make his point when I get my exam results; 'Magenta, the Laws of Probability give more credence to me setting up a burger bar on Mars than you ever getting a decent job with these grades!' so I do have a teensy bit of an understanding). Anyway, as the nearest elephant, asthmatic or otherwise, was probably (unfairly) locked up in a compound a couple of hundred miles away and ghosts aren't real (although, if you talk to Belinda, she'll argue the case for the opposition), the chances were that it was probably a homeless person who was seeking asylum in my bedroom.

Now don't get me wrong, I'm very generous when it comes to giving to those less fortunate than myself, but there are limits – and donating my bed (even a hard, lumpy one like this) went way beyond what could reasonably be described as charitable. But, how to get him (or her) out – now that was a tricky one. I mean, there was no guarantee that it was a friendly homeless person, was there? It could be a distinctly *un*friendly homeless person. In fact, when I thought about it – Holden had gone missing and now there was a strange person (with serious body odour) in my room. OK, so my thought processes were probably a teensy bit slower than usual because of all the sun and the trauma of the afternoon, but I put two and two together and – ohmigod!

I'd got the cousin-kidnapper in my chalet! Which probably explained the disgusting smell; it wasn't the abductor who was so pungent, it was the subject of the abduction, the odious oddity himself – Holden!

I didn't know what to do. I needed help. Slowly, I started to back out of the door. Migraine or not, Belinda was the only adult within shrieking distance. But just as I was heading back into the sitting room, there was a deafening noise that scared the life out of me. It was like a cross between a sneeze and whooping cough with a hint of screeching car tyres thrown in – at about a thousand decibels. Eeeek! No way was that made by a human. In fact, I was beginning to think that Belinda might be right about ghosts after all.

I turned to run, but just at that moment I heard movement from the direction of my bed. The thing was getting up. And it was following me.

'AAAAAAGGGGGH!' I yelled at the top of my voice, then tripped over one of my flip-flops, bashed into the door jamb and staggered backwards on to the very bed that the creature was on. 'HELP!' I screamed, as something huge, hairy and foul-breathed bore down on me. 'HELP ME!'

10
Magenta

'Magenta?'

It was hard to make out who was calling to me when I was under attack from the Beast from Beyond, but it definitely sounded both human and familiar – which had got to be a plus.

'Help me!' I screamed again.

'What's going on?' Belinda was standing in the doorway and, even in the shaft of light from the sitting room, I could see she looked about as healthy as Caspar the Ghost. 'Ugh! What on Earth is that awful smell, Magenta?'

Durr! If I knew that, I wouldn't be screaming for help, now would I?

'Something's in my bed,' I whimpered.

She gave an irritated tut. 'What do you mean *something*?'

Again – durr! If I knew what that *something* was, I wouldn't be saying *something* – I would be telling her exactly *what* was in my bed.

'And it would help if you put the light on.'

Durr, durr and double durr! Didn't she think I'd

already thought of that? Being almost fourteen is not another word for being stupid – well, almost fourteen is two words really, but either way, it doesn't mean I'm brainless. But before I could answer, the monster let out another gruff snort, only this time it was much clearer.

'Eeee-aw!' And, just in case we were in any doubt, 'Eeee-aw!' again. OK – mystery solved! I didn't need a degree in zoology to work out that my new room-mate was none other than a donkey!

'What are you doing with a donkey in your room, Magenta?' I could just make out that Belinda had her hand over her nose and mouth, as though she was going to chuck any minute. 'Take it out; it's terribly unhygienic.'

Er – hello! Had she just missed the last two minutes of conversation?

'I didn't put it here,' I pointed out – which I would have thought would've been fairly obvious, if she'd been paying attention. Although to give her the benefit of the doubt, she really did look rough.

'Then how did it get here?' Good question. 'Although, right now, I'm not interested. Just, please,' she wafted her hand over her nose and turned back to her own room, 'get rid of it. I'm sure its owners must be out there looking for it.'

Now that I knew the demon in the duvet wasn't some psychopathic, child-eating, soul-sucking, cousin-kidnapping hellhound, I felt fairly safe to go past it and turn on the bedside lamp. If I was expected to take the thing back to its owners, I needed to at least be able to see what I was doing. But as I was edging my way round its enormous head – which would've been quite sweet, actually, if it hadn't been so disgustingly smelly – my foot caught on something sticking out from under Justine's bed. And then I realised (speaking of psychopathic hellhounds) that the donkey wasn't the only missing pet in my room that night.

'Get out of there, you little toerag.' I reached down and grabbed hold of the size-two sandal that was just visible in the crack of light from the doorway. Then I yanked it hard, dragging Holden out from under his sister's bed.

'Ouch!' the nauseating little nerd yelled. 'Gerroff me! I might get trampled on.' If only!

'Out! Now!' I grabbed him by the arm and pulled him to his feet. 'OK – Donkey Kong – walk! There are some people who will be very interested to hear what you've got to say about all this.'

I took Holden in one hand and the donkey's reins in the other and marched them back to the HQ of

Operation Missing Link. Well, when I say marched, it was more like heaved them really – donkeys don't get a reputation for being stubborn for no reason – and believe me, the donkey wasn't the only one dragging its hooves along the path between the chalets – I'm surprised there was any concrete left, Holden put up such a struggle.

Now, I wasn't exactly expecting a reward for finding the disappearing duo, but a thank you wouldn't have gone amiss. Instead – talk about the return of the prodigal son! If I'd done something as stupid as donkey-napping, I'd have been in solitary confinement for the rest of my natural life, but not my maggot-featured cousin. Oh no! Auntie Heather nearly smothered him as she clutched him to her floral bosom and rained kisses on him. Ewww – gross! I'd just told her where he'd been! Even the police officers only gave him a ticking-off and told him not to do anything like that again – can you believe it? And, of course, guess who ended up getting this one dumped on her as well as everything else that's gone wrong on this holiday?

'After Magenta made all the donkeys scared . . .' was the opening line of his defence.

It turns out that when I *accidentally* (a little word that everyone seems to be conveniently forgetting) steered my parasail into the donkeys on the beach, one of them had run off into the sand dunes where Holden was hiding from Justine. The donkey, no doubt recognising a kindred spirit, took a fancy to my mule-faced cousin and the two of them were having a whale of a time, until the minuscule Dr Evil decided it would be really funny to sneak his new playmate into our room and hide it there till we got back. Great joke – not! Especially with half the Norfolk constabulary out there on full alert.

Apparently, when Dad and Belinda got back after the court hearing, they hadn't closed the door properly and while Dad was settling Belinda into bed with her migraine, the pongy pair had sneaked in without being seen – or, more amazingly, smelled!

'And didn't anyone stop you on your way through the camp?' Uncle Wayne asked.

Holden shook his head. 'I took him round the back of all the buildings. No one even saw us.'

You see – didn't I say it was a bad thing that we were stuck out on the edge of the campsite? The only good thing to come out of all this is that, because of the smell (and the disgusting pile of donkey-poo – gross!) in our bedroom, we've been moved to another chalet – and it's an upgrade! Yeah!

We now have a bath – and a TV with a remote! How cool is that?

Oops! It seems there are several downsides to having a platinum-grade wooden hut, as opposed to the old silver-category one:

1) The beds in this chalet are on the acceptable side of comfortable, which meant that we all overslept this morning, and that meant that half Gran's family missed her birthday breakfast! Still, burned muesli and soggy toast is hardly the most appetising food for a birthday bash – I'm sure we'll make up for it this afternoon. We're all going for a beach picnic – well away from the water sports and donkeys, I hope!

2) I could've sworn I saw that Liam guy from Leeds lurking round the corner as I went to the camp shop to buy a cereal bar (because I'd missed out on the burned muesli and soggy toast extravaganza earlier). I'd only gone about a hundred metres when I realised I'd left my purse, but as soon as I turned round, I caught a glimpse of him ducking back behind the end chalet, like he'd been following me or something. Weird!

And,

3) It's miles from Uncle Wayne's chalet where Daniel is *still* not speaking to me. He's not even answering my calls. I don't know what I'm supposed to have done – after all, it was *him* who walked off and left me yesterday, so by rights, it should be *me* who's peed off with *him*. I suppose that's why they say girls are more mature than boys, because I'd forgiven him ages ago.

Justine was all, 'Don't worry, Magenta, I'll go and talk to Danno and try to find out what's going on with him.' Gggrrr! Like she's Dr Phil or someone.

'It's fine, thanks, Justine. If Daniel wants to sulk, I'm not going to pander to his childish behaviour. Do you fancy trying out our routine for Friday?' It was only two days to the talent show and, I must be honest, Justine and I hadn't practised our Christina Aguilera song at all.

Then she hit me with bombshell number one. 'Actually, Mum and I have been thinking and we've decided I'd be better off doing a solo.'

'What! But we agreed.'

'No, Magenta, you agreed. I'm going to do "Stupid Girls" by Pink.' Well, that figures! 'I did it in an end-of-term review at school, so I don't need to rehearse it much.'

Talk about selfish. 'Fine, then. I'll just go and find Spud, see if he wants to hang out.'

But then she dropped bombshell number two. 'Actually, Spud, Danno and I have arranged to go on the go-karts this morning.' Oh great! You see what I mean about her brainwashing people? She's now got Spud under her evil spell too. 'Why don't you ask Mum if she'd like a hand making the picnic for this afternoon? She's got a tonne of chicken slices in their mini-fridge. Let's face it, it's a crap job but someone's got to do it. See you!'

'Whatever!' I shouted as she flounced out of our new platinum-range chalet.

Help Auntie Heather make sandwiches? Yeah right! On my list of a ka-trillion things I never want to do – ever – is spending a baking hot morning with the auntie from hell, putting lumps of dead hen between bread.

But it was beginning to look like I had no choice. The rest of my family were all busy: Dad had taken Belinda to the medical centre because her migraine still wasn't any better; Uncle Wayne had taken Holden to the adventure playground and Auntie Venice had taken Gran for a birthday manicure and facial.

So, that just left me – but if my conniving cousin

thought she could turn me into Nelly No-mates, she could think again. There was no way I was going to take this lying down. I grabbed my shades and headed for the go-kart track. Forgiven or not, I wanted some answers from Daniel and I wanted them now!

'Daniel!' I tried to flag him down as he hurtled round the track. I was peering through the chain-link fence, watching and waving, but he wasn't taking any notice. He had his hands on this tiny little steering wheel and you could see the concentration on his face as he turned it to avoid the stacks of old tyres and bales of straw that were positioned all round the sides. He looked so sweet, actually. He was wearing a crash helmet and he'd got this sort of motor-racing suit on, but he'd rolled down the top half so that he didn't have anything above his waist – and talk about phwoar! Oh my God! Daniel was seriously hot! He had muscles and ripples and a six pack and everything. I mean, I'd seen him on the beach and stuff, but this was different; he was being all manly and looking extremely Grand Prix. In fact, I don't think I'm exaggerating when I tell you – my boyfriend is a hunk! How come I'd never noticed this about him before? Or, more to the point, why hadn't he shown me that he had an upper body to die for? And why does he suddenly start stripping off and flaunting it the minute I'm out of the picture? It was quite obvious that he was trying to impress Justine with his physique. Well, I might have been peed off with him but I hadn't actually dumped him (yet) and, as far as I was aware, I hadn't been dumped by him – officially. So that meant he was still my boyfriend. Although not for long, I can tell you. I wanted a serious word with him.

'DANIEL!' I was jumping up and down and screaming at the top of my voice as he came round the track again and headed up the straight, towards me.

At last! He looked up and saw me. But then – oops, oh no! The expression on his face turned from one of concentration to one of shock and, before you could say Jenson Button, the go-kart careered right off the mini-road, over the little rubber barrier, and smashed headlong into the biggest pile of tyres.

Uh-oh! As Daniel clambered out of his go-kart he was holding his head. Men in black boiler suits were running towards him and I was beginning to think that I wasn't going to come out of this looking good – again! I'm sick of getting blamed for everything, so

I backed off. Maybe I needed to rethink my plans for the morning.

Which would've been OK, if my new plans had included finding myself a stalker! I decided that a spell on the beach on my own would give me some space to clear my head. And, who knows, maybe if I kept my distance from Daniel, he'd realise what he was missing? You know, absence making the heart grow fonder and all that.

But, it didn't matter where I went, because every time I looked round that loony Liam was following me; when I went to get supplies of chocolate from the camp supermarket, there he was dodging down behind the doughnuts; as I was sunbathing on the beach, he just happened to be bending down and picking something out of the sand and, when I got back to camp (because, I must be honest, it was a teensy bit boring on the beach on my own), Liam was there, crouching down behind the chairlift terminal.

Actually, it was starting to creep me out a bit. I know my friends accused me of stalking Adam Jordan once, but that was entirely different:

1) I only ever stalked him because I liked him and thought that if I could get him to notice me, he'd like me too.

2) It only happened once – ish.

3) He did end up noticing me – only not in a good way, because I fell into a dustbin behind his house and then nearly got run over.

And,

4) He turned out to be a jerk anyway so wasn't even worth it in the first place.

But this thing with Liam was seriously psycho.

Once I got off the cable car, I legged it back to Auntie Heather's chalet; any port in a storm, as they say. And if making sandwiches with the Witch of Wilmslow was my only protection against the Leeds liability, then dead hens it was. The problem was, when I got there, Daniel was also there – and, after his accident on the go-karts, we now have three members of our party in neck braces! Oops. The medical centre will have to have a restock at this rate.

Oh boy! What a day. I managed to put on a brave face for Gran but this afternoon was the worst one – ever!

a) Daniel is even more not speaking to me – if that's possible when he wasn't speaking to me in the first place. But now he's not speaking to me *and* giving me nasty looks, which is even worse than simply not speaking because . . . well, it just is.

b) Justine is running around after him like she's his own private nursemaid: 'Oooo, you just relax, I'll get you some more Coke, Danno,' and 'You can rest your head on my legs if it makes the pain any less, Danno,' and, 'You mustn't lift things, so I'll just hold those really heavy crisps for you and drop them into your mouth – like I was your girlfriend – *Danno*!' Ggggrrr!

c) Spud's gone off with his parents for the afternoon because he thought the picnic should be a family occasion, so I was all on my own till Dad took pity on me and coaxed me into a game of Frisbee with him. The trouble is, I've never been that good at throwing, and the Frisbee slipped out of my hand on the second throw. And it smacked Auntie Vee right in the mouth, knocking her false teeth out. You would not believe how quickly things sink into this sand. Honestly, we were all searching and digging practically as soon as she'd stopped writhing about and we'd mopped up the blood with our towels, but we only found her top set – and that was in two halves. She's sitting there sulking, like one of those African tribeswomen who have plates in their lip – except she hasn't got a plate, she hasn't even got teeth – it's just the swelling that's made her lip big. I wasn't expecting much of a birthday present from her this year anyway – what with the whole swimming pool/whiplash thing – so I guess I can cross her off the list altogether now.

And,

d) I'd no sooner put sunblock on and was going to lie down to sunbathe, than the unspeakable urchin pulled away my lilo so that I fell backwards and ended up looking like a giant piece of sandpaper! Honestly, I was so mad! I'd got half the beach stuck to me and everyone was laughing. I had to go in the sea to wash it off and it was freezing. I hate my cousin – come to think of it, I hate both my cousins! I am so glad I'm an only child.

Anyway, I've moved right away from them all now. I've taken my lilo to the other side of Kiddies' Corner – so no one can come near me, or bother me, or blame me for anything else. I've had enough of all of them. I've found myself a nice little spot near the cliffs and I'm just going to lie here and rest till it's time to go back. Then I think I'll have an early night. I don't care if it's Gran's birthday. I don't want to go out with them all tonight – I just want to be alone.

Uh-oh! Wait a minute – I know I said I wanted to be alone, but I didn't mean *this* alone. One minute I was sunbathing on the beach and the next, the lilo was bobbing up and down in a very unstable, un-beach-like sort of way.

Oh my God! Now I've opened my eyes, the situation is a zillion times worse than I imagined. There are seagulls flapping about over my head and nothing but water all around me. The beach is like a little yellow strip on the horizon – and it's getting further and further away.

Help! The tide must have come in and washed me away. Now I'm heading for Holland without a paddle and no one even realises that I'm missing!

11
Daniel

This is turning out to be about as much fun as a scuba diving holiday with the Barracuda Family – in concrete flippers – and probably only half as dangerous. Which isn't being fair to Spud or Justine, because they've tried really hard to cheer me up and keep my mind occupied, but the bottom line is, without Magenta, my life just isn't the same. I don't want to go anywhere or do anything.

It's not like I want us to be joined at the hip, but just knowing that she's my girlfriend and I can tell her things makes all the difference. When we're OK together, all the time I'm thinking, *when I see Magenta, I'll tell her about this* – or that, or whatever's going on for me. But when we're not getting on, it's like there's a huge void in my life – and my heart. I don't want to be round other people, watching them having fun and trying to be all happy with them. The only thing I want is to be by myself. I know that sounds really sad, especially after the way Magenta's treated me, but the simple truth is: I love her and I want to be with her.

When I saw her standing by the go-kart track and waving to me, it was as though on all the previous circuits I'd been on autopilot, but as soon as she appeared, it was like someone had pumped life into me and there was this bhangra beat going on in my chest. We've got a group of kids in our school who have a dhol drumming club and, believe me, when I saw Magenta standing at the other side of the mesh, my heart rate wouldn't have been out of place at their end-of-term concert.

I was just coming up the back straight for the fourth time when she caught my eye. Wow! She looked so beautiful and sophisticated, standing there in her shades, she took my breath away. I was pretty sure she was calling to me, although after everything that Justine and that creep Liam had said, I wanted to make absolutely certain that it was my name she was calling and not Spud's.

Spud had told me there was nothing going on between them. 'Neh! I don't know where Juss got that from. She dumped *me* for *you* – remember?' But I wanted to be sure.

So I looked up and (oh deep joy!) her lips (those wonderfully soft and kissable lips) were definitely forming the word, 'Daniel.' I was so happy; I wanted to jump out of the go-kart on the spot and rush over to her, take her in my arms and kiss her, you know, like they do on those romantic old black and white videos Mum's always putting on her birthday list.

But that was when things started to go arse over elbow – literally! I lost concentration for about a nanosecond and before I knew what was happening – bam! I'd missed the corner and smashed straight into one of the buffers. Whoa! It was a hell of a shock. I don't know what it must be like for those Formula One guys when they crash because, believe me, I wouldn't want to do this again in a hurry. I was totally disorientated for a minute or so and my head felt like it was too heavy for my neck. The guys from the maintenance bay took me off to the medical centre and that was the first disappointment because I was half expecting Magenta to come rushing over to see if I was all right. But she didn't and, when I looked round to see her and give her the thumbs-up that I was OK, she was heading off towards the shopping area. But worse still, that creep Liam was running after her.

'What happened, man?' Spud came over to me.

'Nothing – I just overshot the corner. No big deal.'

I wasn't going to tell anyone what a fool I'd been – again! What was I thinking, to have even imagined that she'd come over to make up with me? I think the sun must've got to me and I'd been deluding myself.

The doctor at the medical centre was trying to be really funny. She gave me a foam collar like the ones Heather and Venice are wearing. 'Well, young man, nothing broken or sprained but your neck muscles have had quite a jolt and might be a bit sore for a while. It's a good job you're fit and healthy. It's probably best to wear this for a couple of days, just to give your neck a rest from carrying around that bulging brain of yours.'

Ho ho ho!

I offered to go off with Spud's family this afternoon, on the pretext that Florence's birthday should be a family affair, but she wouldn't hear of it.

'Nonsense! You came with us on this holiday as part of the family and I want you at my celebration. I've known you since you were born, and I used to child-mind you when you were little, so I'd be deeply hurt if you didn't turn up. And I don't want any presents either – just your company.'

So that was it then; happy families on the beach. Not that I could do much. My neck was really starting to stiffen up. Every time I tried to turn to speak to Magenta it hurt like hell and I ended up grimacing – hope she didn't think I was pulling faces at her. In the end, I just lay down and decided to take the opportunity for some serious R and R.

Of course Justine was smarming up to me: 'Oh, Danno, would you like me to rub sunblock on for you?'

And she was even trying to feed me crisps like I was some sort of baby. She was all, 'I know Magenta's family and everything, but honestly, Danno, you're worth so much more. Why do you let her treat you like that? You should find someone else to go out with this holiday and really show her that you have more respect for yourself than she obviously has for you.'

I'm not stupid – I know Juss would really like it for her and me to get it on again but, even though she looks a bit like Magenta – she's not her. I didn't want to be too rude because, well, to be honest, I didn't have the energy. So, in the end, I just let her get on with it. She was pushing these crisps into my mouth – I don't even like prawn cocktail flavour – and rabbiting on about Magenta. Of course, what was even more annoying than Justine was that, as the tide was coming in, we had to keep moving our things back up towards the sand dunes. And every time I stood up, it felt like the muscles down each side of my neck were being ripped apart. The doctor had given me some painkillers but I think they must have worn off.

At one point, I'd been lying down for a while, just trying to numb out from what was going on:

a) in my neck area and

b) with Magenta.

She'd taken her lilo and walked off and I hadn't seen her for about an hour. I know the doctor made a joke about my 'bulging brains' but it didn't take more than a couple of brain cells to work out that she'd sneaked off to meet her new holiday romance – Lurking Liam – and I couldn't bear thinking about it. I think I might even have drifted off to sleep for a while when, suddenly, there were these two deafening bangs, like a couple of bombs going off.

I tried to sit up quickly. 'Ow, ow, ow!' A bit too quickly, actually. But once I'd managed to manoeuvre myself into an, almost, sitting position, I leaned over in the general direction of Curtis. 'What the hell was that?' What a perfect way to round off this holiday, finding ourselves in the middle of a war zone!

'The maroons,' he said, picking up his binoculars and looking round, vaguely distracted.

'The what?' Holden the hobgoblin piped up.

But, actually, I'm glad he asked because I hadn't a clue what Curtis was on about. It's one thing to have a daughter named after a colour, but when you start calling sounds dark red too, then I was starting to think I wasn't the only one who'd been out in the sun too long.

'Maroons,' he repeated anxiously, as he put the binoculars to his eyes and scanned the beach. 'They're like distress flares with loud bangs. The coastguard sets them off to alert the lifeboat crew. When they hear the maroons, it's a signal for them to drop everything and dash to the lifeboat. It means someone's in distress at sea.' He started to bite his bottom lip. 'Speaking of which, has anyone seen Magenta recently?'

Belinda tugged on his arm. 'Sit down and don't be silly. Other people have accidents too, you know. Magenta's not at the centre of *every* disaster.' She turned and glared at Heather who was in the deckchair next to hers.

Heather didn't even open her eyes. Without turning her head, she said, 'We'll see.'

And sure enough, two seconds later, we saw!

Curtis threw down his binoculars. 'Oh, good God! It *is* her. Help! Help! My daughter's out there. Help her someone!' He began leaping down the beach like a gazelle, or, to be more accurate, a wildebeest, in swim shorts.

'Oh my Lord! Stop him!' Florence flapped her hand in Curtis's direction. 'Go after him, Wayne. You know he only got as far as the bronze medal when he did personal survival! I don't want to lose a son *and* a granddaughter on my birthday!'

'Don't worry, Mum. I'll get him.' Wayne legged it down the beach after his brother.

Magenta was in distress out at sea so it didn't matter how much distress I was in on land, I had to go to her. I had to save her. But just when I needed to be at my fittest, I was having difficulty even struggling to my feet.

'Wait for me!' I called to Curtis and Wayne.

'She'll be fine,' Justine said, dismissively. 'She always is.'

I was furious! My beautiful Magenta was in danger and her cousin was still being a bitch towards her. 'You just don't get it, do you, Justine?' It felt like I had a thousand red-hot pins piercing my neck every time I moved, but I braved the pain. 'I love Magenta!'

She shrugged and turned back to her magazine. 'Whatever floats your boat.'

I just hoped that someone, even if it wasn't me,

could keep Magenta's boat afloat – or lilo, or whatever it was she was on, till the lifeboat got to her. But the way I waddled down the beach, trying to keep my neck straight, I was about as agile as a limbless crab. How could such a relatively tiny little piece of anatomy like my neck have such a major effect on every other part of my body? There was no point in the doctor telling me I was fit and healthy, when every step I took made me feel (and probably look) about a hundred and ten.

By the time I got to the edge of the sea, Curtis and Wayne were standing next to each other, gnawing their nails and gazing out to where a tiny yellow dot was bobbing up and down on the horizon, drifting off into infinity.

'Aren't you going to save her?' I asked, horrified that they could stand back and let my Magenta disappear into the distance. If I didn't have this foam brace on my neck – which, let's face it, would absorb so much water it would've been about as buoyant as lead water wings – I would've swum to the moon to rescue her.

'No point in trying to swim out to her, Daniel; better to wait for the lifeboat,' Wayne told me. He had his hand on Curtis's arm, holding him back.

'Anyway . . .' He pointed in the direction of a

blob of black hair getting further and further out from the land, dipping and rising with the waves. 'It's the kid from the pool. He's going to swim out and wait with her till the lifeboat gets there. He said he was a strong swimmer and he's got lifesaving medals,' he explained.

Oh great! Liam the leech! Why wasn't I surprised? Didn't I say she'd probably been with him this afternoon when she'd walked off? He'd been sticking to her like a limpet all week and, apparently, she'd been dishing out kisses 'liberally' at every opportunity. I was just gobsmacked that Curtis could've let him go after her when he's known what the jerk was like from the first day.

'I'll leave you to it, then,' I said, turning back and hobbling up the beach. I went back to the women who were waiting anxiously. 'Could I have the key please, Mrs Orange?' I asked Heather. 'I'd just like to go back and rest. My neck's killing me.'

'I can come with you if you like,' Justine offered.

'Get out of my face, Juss!' I know it sounded harsh, but why couldn't she get the message?

Heather lifted up her sunglasses and was just about to say something – and from the set of her eyes, I don't think it was going to be complimentary.

'Sorry,' I said. 'It's just that my neck's really playing up.'

Heather let her glasses drop back on to her nose and handed me the key. 'You're not the only one with a bad neck, you know, Daniel. Honestly, youngsters today just don't have the pain tolerance of our generation, do they, Venice?'

'Wimps, that's what they are; utter wimps!' Venice lisped through her swollen lips.

Oh great! Any more for the Daniel-bashing bandwagon? Now I knew what my namesake felt like when he was thrown into the lion's den!

'Aren't you going to wait and see that Magenta's all right?' Belinda asked.

I would've shaken my head if I could've managed it. 'The lifeboat's on its way. I'm sure she'll be fine.'

Why would I want to stay and see her being given mouth-to-mouth from Mr Liberal Lips himself – Liam from Leeds? Didn't she realise I was in enough pain as it was? I headed back to the chalet.

To make matters worse, tomorrow's the Master Hay's Holiday Competition that Spud wanted us both to enter. I'm not really into these big-orexia type contests, but I am quite proud of my body at the moment so I'd fancied my chances. But there's no way I can go in for it now. How could I enter a fitness competition looking like an advert for Injury Lawyers 4 U?

So, as if the situation with Magenta isn't bad enough, this neck thing is really starting to get to me. In fact, the only things that really appeal to me at this moment are:

1) Digging a big hole in the sand and burying myself in it – but the irony is, my neck's so painful I couldn't even pick up a spade.

2) Swimming out to sea and not stopping till I reached France – but again, I refer to the whole foam collar/lead water wings scenario.

Or, failing those:

3) Catching a bus (or a train, or even a rickshaw) home – but even if I knew where to catch one from, once I got back, the keys to our house are locked up next door and I can't really see Curtis letting me go off with his keys when Mum put him in charge of looking after me. And on that subject – great job, Curtis! I've ended up with a strained neck, a broken heart and a severely punctured ego – way to go! Of course, I could go to Dad's but Joe's there and he'd only take the piss out of me – which Magenta's already doing very nicely, thank you very much!

But there's only two more days left. And, on the positive side, at least having a busted neck means I won't be able to go in for the talent contest with Spud, on Friday. Yes! Actually, when I think about it, that's a pretty big plus and it's cheered me up a bit. I might go and get myself a pizza before they come back and start droning on about how amazing Liam is and how he managed to rescue Magenta and where would they be without him and wouldn't he like to join their family and move in with them. Hurl, hurl! Suddenly, I've gone off the idea of pizza. Think I'll just give Spud a ring and see if he wants to hang out for a bit.

12
Magenta

I've got two questions:

1) What part of 'Leave me alone!' does Liam *not* understand? And,

2) What *is* the matter with Daniel? (Apart from his neck – obviously.) He can't even look at me now. I wouldn't mind but I've done absolutely nothing to him at all – well, apart from maybe distracting him a teensy little bit when he crashed his go-kart. But really, is that enough to make him carry on like he doesn't even know me?

But let me talk you through them one at a time. First of all, the matter of the loony from Leeds:

There I was drifting across the North Sea with only a very flimsy piece of plastic between me and an extremely watery death, when whose head should pop up between the waves than that psycho-nutter, Liam! Honestly, I think we're talking serious insanity here.

'Well, well, well, if it isn't Little Miss Teaser,' he

said, grabbing hold of my lilo and almost tipping me into the sea.

'What?'

I thought he must be confusing me with Justine, but oh no – he soon made it very clear that he'd got the right cousin.

'How do you like it when people mess with you – Magenta?' he said, shaking the lilo till I nearly fell off.

Yikes! I thought the diving board incident was scary enough but this had a fear factor that was off the scales.

'What do you want?' I screamed, clinging on to the airbed like my life depended on it – which, when you think about it, it did!

'Not so funny now, is it?' And he gave it another shake.

'What *is* wrong with you?' I yelled. Had he any idea how long it had taken me to straighten my hair this morning? If I ended up in the water it'd go all frizzy again. 'Just leave me alone.'

'OK,' he smirked, then bobbed down under the waves.

Phew! I could see the lifeboat heading towards me and was just beginning to feel a teensy bit relieved when, suddenly, the whole lilo was lifted in the air. The fruitcake had only gone and decided that now was a good time to do his Jaws impersonation. He came up underneath the airbed and tipped it up. I was tossed right off it and into the water.

'Aaaagh!' If that was his idea of leaving me alone, I'd hate to see him if he was full on in someone's face.

When I came to the surface my hair was plastered all over my eyes – at least I hoped it was my hair. I tried to push it away but – oh gross – there was something disgustingly slimy sticking to my head. Eww!

'You . . . ugh . . . moron!' I was clinging to the lilo with one hand and treading water to keep afloat. 'What . . . ugh . . . the hell . . . is . . . ugh . . . wrong with . . . ugh . . . you?' I've always prided myself on my ability to multitask, so while I was clinging to the wreckage of my lilo and having a go at Lamebrain Liam, I was also attempting to simultaneously spit out the half litre of North Sea I'd swallowed in the capsize *and* discover what it was that had attached itself to me. And doing a pretty good job, I thought. Until – uh-oh!

Ohmigod, ohmigod, ohmigod! It was a giant jellyfish and it was trying to suck my brains out! Help!

OK, panic over. I pulled a lump of evil-looking seaweed off my head and was more than a teensy bit relieved to see that it wasn't a jellyfish, giant or otherwise. Another massive sigh of relief! Although, the more I pulled the more I realised that it wasn't just one lump that had drifted there on its own; it had brought its entire family with it and taken up residence in my hair. How disgusting is that! Honestly, when I think of the length of time I'd spent washing and drying and straightening and glittering, only to end up looking like I was wearing some grotesque *Pirates of the Caribbean* sea-monster type wig! I promised myself that if I came out of this alive, I was going to make Liam sorry he'd ever set eyes on me. But, actually, I was beginning to think that the first part of that sentence was by no means a forgone conclusion.

'Oh dear, that was careless of you,' Liam sneered. 'Better hold tight to your lilo now. We don't want you drowning, do we? Oh, look, the plug's come out. I hope it doesn't deflate before the lifeboat gets here.'

Seriously, the guy is off his trolley!

But the worst thing was, when the lifeboat did reach me, Liam flung one arm round my chest and cupped my chin in his other hand like he was rescuing me. He shouted up to the men in the boat, 'Good to see you, guys. I've been keeping her afloat for you.'

Once we were on board they were all over him like he was some sort of superhero and one man was even talking about nominating him for a medal! Can you believe it? I was thinking of trying to get my own back, but on second thoughts, Liam is sooooo scary, he's positively certifiable. So I've decided to keep a low profile and stay well out of his way till we go home.

And speaking of certifiable idiots, that brings me to the other headcase in my life at the moment: Daniel! He is being too weird for words. Now, I realise that this holiday hasn't been quite the romantic interlude we'd both hoped and I am beginning to think that we're over. But (and I know I might be labouring the point here), neither of us has actually spoken those two little words, 'You're dumped' yet – so, technically, I am still his girlfriend. And, according to *my* rules, that means he should either speak to me or finish with me. But, honestly, I might as well have donned my cloak of invisibility for all the notice he's taking of me. He walks straight past me without even blinking and he doesn't answer any of my questions – not even the nice ones like, 'How's your neck?' Mind you, the only consolation is, he's not talking to Justine either.

'Trust me; you're better off without him, Madge,' she said.

I gave Justine one of my looks. Like, hello! Who does she think she is, calling me Madge? Only my best friends, Seema and Arlette, are allowed to call me that. But I didn't say anything. In fact (and I never thought you'd hear me say this) it was quite nice that Justine and I were on speaking terms again. I'd spent so much time on my own this holiday I was beginning to lose the power of communication.

We were sitting in the camp theatre waiting for the Master Hay's Holidays Contest so that we could offer moral support to Spud and Holden. (Don't even go there – it was Auntie Heather's idea to enter him.) Although, I wasn't sure how *moral* the whole business of boys showing off their bodies was. I'd tried to quiz Belinda on any possible ethical grounds for objecting to the whole principle, but Dad warned me that if I got into any more trouble he would cancel my birthday. Which definitely put a different slant on things and made me realise that, ethically and morally, my birthday was more important than a load of stupid boys flexing their muscles.

But, even though we'd gone there for the sole purpose of cheering on the lads, Daniel was still ignoring us. Justine and I were sitting right at the front when he walked in. He was still wearing his collar and, actually, he looked so sweet – like a cute little chick popping his head out of a foam egg.

'Hi, Daniel, we've saved you a seat,' I said. But he just walked on by – like I didn't exist. And he went and sat at the back all on his own.

'Seriously, move on,' Justine advised me.

And (this makes two things I never thought you'd hear me say) – I think she's right! So, as from now, I am officially moving on with my life.

The Master Hay's Holidays competition was pretty boring, actually. Justine was all, 'Phwoar! Awesome!' But I wasn't impressed. I think if Daniel hadn't been all trussed up like a turkey, he'd have knocked spots off all of them. And the fact that I can say that just shows that I've moved on and don't bear him any resentment for the way he's treated me at all.

Of course I expect you've already guessed that the overall winner was that skunk of a hunk, Liam! (So much for trying to keep out of his way!) But it was no surprise really – even though Liam is definitely of unsound mind, he is of very very sound body indeed! If there was a surprise, it was that the evil grub came in third in the under tens category. I can only assume that the judges were either blind or had been heavily bribed. Of course Auntie Heather was all over him (and the judges) like eczema. Sadly, Spud didn't even get a consolation prize in any category, but he was cool about it.

'You can't win 'em all,' he said. Unfortunately, Spud never wins any of them – only he doesn't seem to have noticed. But, as he's the only one who's speaking to us at the moment, I certainly wasn't going to point it out to him.

Anyway, we're going home tomorrow – and I cannot wait!

1) Even though our chalet got upgraded, the food didn't. Last night Belinda and I queued for fifteen minutes to find that vegetable korma was the only item on the menu that hadn't once had a face. Belinda was a bit iffy (in view of her dodgy-curry food poisoning at the beginning of the week) but she needn't have worried – this tasted less like curry and more like a tin of slime soup poured over congealed rice. Yuk!

2) It means I'll never have to see that creep Liam again. And, believe me, even that's too soon. You should've seen him strutting round the

stage when he won. His head's so big, I'm surprised he can lift it off the floor.

3) Once I'm back on my home territory with my *true* friends around me for support, I can dump Daniel properly and really start to get on with my life.

And, most importantly:

4) It's only two days to my birthday! Yay!

But in the meantime, there's this evening's un-exciting, un-fun, un-interesting, non-entertainment to look forward to: the family talent show. Great!

After Justine decided to go it alone, I was left with several choices:

a) I could've done my impression of Christina Aguilera on my own, but as I don't know all the words to any of her songs, I'd probably have looked a total dork.

b) I could have been a Cheeky Girl (note the singular) but that seemed even sadder.

Or,

c) I could have tried to remember the routine I learned to 'The Surrey With the Fringe on Top' when my dancing class did *Oklahoma* when I was eight.

So, in the end I decided not to enter. Which I think was probably one of my better decisions this holiday. The contestants had to get there early for sound checks and hair and make-up – which actually sounded quite exciting and I had a momentary pang of regret about not entering, but I soon got over it. So Justine, Holden (who's going to perform a comedy magic show – don't get me started!) and Spud all left the chalets at about six. Which left me in the fun-filled company of the adults – and not forgetting Mr Laugh-a-minute, Daniel. Great! To give Dad his due, he did try to liven things up a bit by taking everyone out to one of the bars before the show. But, as Daniel was glued to his Nintendo DS, I was left in the scintillating world of 'Grown-up Talk': the education system, house prices and the government. Honestly, I'm not surprised adults lose their marbles as they get older. They really need to find more stimulating topics of conversation. Although Auntie Heather did try to take the discussion in a different direction – moaning about Gran and Auntie Venice – again!

She was sitting there with a face like a sucked lemon. 'Honestly, Wayne, they're her own grandchildren and she can't even be bothered to turn up to support them. She's your mother – do something.'

It seems the golden oldies had offended her by

preferring to go to bingo than watch her dear little cherubs in the talent show – can't say I blame them, to be honest.

'Like what?' Poor Uncle Wayne. 'She's seventy years old, I'm sure she's capable of making up her mind about what she wants to do on her last evening and if she doesn't want to spend it watching a load of amateurs making prats of themselves, then that's her choice.' Good on you, Uncle Wayne!

'Wayne!' Auntie Heather nearly choked on her port and lemon. 'May I remind you, that those *prats* you're talking about include your children!' Never a truer word spoken! She folded her arms and sat in a huff for the rest of the evening.

Unfortunately, her bad mood hadn't worn off by the time we eventually made our way into the theatre. She practically trampled over a group of pensioners, elbowing them out of her path, in a bid for front seats.

'Over here!' she screeched, flapping her flowery chiffon scarf in the air to attract Dad and Uncle Wayne's attention. 'I've got us six seats right in the middle of the front row. Oi, you! They're taken!' she shrieked at an elderly man on a Zimmer frame who tried to sit down next to her.

The talent show was like everything else on this holiday – and I include my love life in that – a complete let-down!

a) Justine was less like Pink and more like Sludge-Grey! I don't know why Uncle Wayne and Auntie Heather have been wasting their money giving her singing lessons; she'd do better as a bird-scarer. Honestly, I don't remember her being that bad when we did our Cheeky Girls routine for the family a few years ago. I thought it was only boys whose voices broke but hers sounds like it's in about a thousand pieces.

b) The only comedy in Holden's comedy-magic act was Holden himself. It's just a shame he couldn't make himself disappear – now that would've been worth watching!

c) Of course halfway through the evening Liam took centre stage to do his version of Eminem. Yeah right – never mind Marshall Mathers, more like Mad Maniac!

And just when I thought things couldn't get any worse, one of the orange-coated camp entertainers came on to make an announcement.

'Before our next act which is a Prodigy tribute band . . .' Oh, this I *had* to see! Who on Earth would try to act like The Prodigy? I mean, spiky hair and mad eye make-up was one thing (well, two, actually) but all those piercings – gross! And then a thought struck me – oh no! Please don't let Justine be having a second go! I don't think I could stand it.

The orange-coat went on, '. . . I have an announcement to make. We have a special someone in our audience tonight . . .' Oh lucky someone! I'd always wanted to have my name read out on TV or the radio. '. . . A certain little lady called Magenta . . .' Wow! How amazing was that? There must be two of us here. I started looking round, wondering what my namesake looked like? '. . . whose birthday it is on Sunday.'

Eeek! OK, enough of the wondering. I was pretty sure there couldn't have been two Magentas who both had birthdays in two days' time. Which meant that the announcement must be for me. Oh wow! And then another thought struck me; it couldn't be, could it? Had Daniel got the compere to apologise on his behalf and declare his love for me publicly? You know, like some people ask their girlfriends to marry them on the TV or at football games. Not that I've ever been to a football game, you understand, but I've seen it happen on films and it is sooooooo romantic. Was this why he'd been so quiet all evening – because he was hoping to lead me off the scent? I leaned forward to try and catch a glimpse of Daniel and give him a smile to let him know that I appreciated how lovely I thought it was, but he was just staring straight ahead like he was on Planet Zog or something.

'Where is Magenta? Is she here?' the man in the orange jacket asked the audience.

'Yes! It's me!' I called out, waving my arms. 'I'm here!' And a spotlight swooped down and shone right on me. How celeb is that?

'Let's have a big hand for Magenta, ladies and gentlemen. And if you'd all like to join me in singing . . . Happy birthday to you. Happy Birthday to you . . .'

A spotlight *and* an entire theatre singing me happy birthday! Did I have the best boyfriend in the universe, or what? I kept looking along the row to try and catch Daniel's eye but he was looking in the completely opposite direction, like he was nothing to do with it. Still, never mind. I expect he was a bit embarrassed in front of the adults, but I'd make sure I thanked him properly later.

When the crowd had finished singing they all clapped and then the MC looked directly at me and said, 'So, Magenta, a very happy fourteenth birthday from the next act . . .'

Uh-oh – the next act? That meant there was no way it was Daniel who requested it. Oh no! There was only one person that I knew who was still left to perform – and that was Spud! I should have known. Ggggrr! I'll kill him when I get hold of him.

But the guy went on, 'So let's have a big hand for Magenta's grandmother – Florence the Firestarter!'

What! With that, loud electronic music blasted across the auditorium and the curtains opened to reveal Gran in her red leathers. Her hair was jelled into little pointed twists that made her head look like some medieval torture ball and she had make-up that was obviously done by Justine. She had more chains dangling off her than a red leather Christmas tree and she was brandishing the microphone like it was a Samurai sword.

'I'm a firestarter, twisted firestarter . . .' Oh my God! Kill me now – please, just put an end to my misery.

But then Auntie Vee only jumped out of the side curtain on to the stage too, all decked out in ripped jeans and safety pins, with spikes sticking out of her surgical collar. And she joined in with Gran. 'You're the firestarter, twisted firestarter . . .'

I had to get out of there. In the last week I'd faced death: falling out of a car, on the diving boards, from the parasail and then the lilo incident, but this was the worst of all – death by slow and excruciating public humiliation. It would have been bad enough if I could've pretended I didn't know them but they'd made sure everyone in the entire camp knew that I had the same DNA. I would never live it down. They'd be staring at me as soon as the lights went up – and again tomorrow at breakfast; all finger-pointing and sniggering. Oh this was too much.

'Just off to the loo,' I whispered to Auntie Heather, and I was out of there. Before they'd got to the second verse, I was out of the door and halfway down the path towards the chalets.

I was just contemplating putting myself up for adoption (which was starting to become a bit of a habit!) when it occurred to me that I hadn't got a key to the chalet – great! So, there I was; nine o'clock at night; pitch dark and nowhere to go. I hadn't even got any money on me. Oh well, there was nothing else for it – I'd just catch the chairlift down to the beach and have a mooch about till it was time for the show to finish.

And, just my luck, as I stood at the cable car docking area waiting for the next chair to swing round so that I could sit in it and get whooshed down to the beach, the hot weather decided to break. I could hear the rumble of thunder in the distance and a big blob of rain plopped on my head. Brilliant! Could life get any worse?

Well, yes, obviously it could.

'So, Miss Fifteen-year-old-independent-traveller – how come your granny thinks you'll only be fourteen on Sunday?' Oops! 'I think someone's been telling porkies.'

As the chairlift caught me behind the knees and swept me up in the air, the loco from Leeds jumped up and plonked himself next to me on the wooden seat. 'I think we should have a little chat, don't you?'

Uh-oh!

13
Daniel

You should've seen Magenta in the theatre. Oh, she looked so beautiful, standing there in the spotlight with a smile on her face like a massive glitter ball that made the whole room sparkle.

Even though I know she's done the dirty on me, it doesn't matter how much I try to deny it – she makes my world turn. It hurt like hell watching her basking in the limelight and knowing that I wasn't part of her life any more. In the end, I couldn't bear to watch. My eyes were welling up and I didn't want everyone thinking I was a total wimp, so I had to look away.

But the minute the theatre stopped singing happy birthday to her, I was shocked back to reality. Florence burst on to the stage, strutting her stuff like a geriatric Little Red Hideous Hood. I know I've always said I quite admired Florence for her eccentricities but even I thought she'd gone too far this time. But to start with, I couldn't draw myself away. It was like watching a car crash – you know you shouldn't be looking but you're glued to it in this sort of mesmerised state of disbelief. Then, out of the corner of my eye, I caught sight of Magenta slipping out of her seat and heading for the exit. I just *knew* she was going to meet up with that slimeball. And – I'm not proud of this, you understand – I followed her. Even as I was going after her, I knew there was something masochistic about it, but I needed actual proof. I needed to see what was going on with my own eyes, instead of just hearing it from Justine or the Letch from Leeds. There was still a part of me that wanted to believe that Magenta wasn't going with him; that there was still a chance for us

I told Curtis that I was going to get a drink. To be honest, I think he'd have liked to have joined me – you should've seen his face when his mother appeared on stage. He dropped his head into his hands and was shaking it like a man who'd lost the will to live. Belinda was patting him on the shoulder in a comforting sort of gesture, although I noticed her eyes were closed and the colour had drained from her face too. In the seats at the other side of them were the other half of the family, and they were in a similar state; Wayne's jaw was trailing on the floor and Heather had adopted the prone position on her seat and was flapping her scarf and pulling at her collar like she was gagging for air. Which was good because it meant that no one was really bothered when I got up and left.

Magenta was a few metres ahead of me but she hadn't even seen me get up. I waited till she'd slipped out of the door and was heading back to the chalets before I sneaked after her, then I made sure I could just keep her within my sights.

The hot weather was starting to break. There was a distant flash followed by the rumble of thunder. I did a mental count, like Mum taught us when we were little, to work out how far away it was: one, two, three, four . . . ten, eleven, twelve! Three miles away. OK, so that wasn't such a problem. The last time Magenta and I had been in a thunderstorm, I'd had to rescue her from a stampeding tent – I certainly didn't want a repeat of that.

I didn't have far to follow her because Magenta's family had been upgraded to a platinum chalet which was right near the centre of the camp – and miles away from where I was having to sleep with the groundhog. When she was almost at her door, she stopped and looked round. Uh-oh! I dodged behind a tree so that she couldn't see me. It was obvious she was looking for Liam. I didn't know why I was doing this. It must be the ultimate self-inflicted torture. From my hiding place I peered along the row of chalets, then back towards the main arena of the camp where the theatre was and, sure enough, there he was about fifty metres behind me – Liam the leech! I *knew* it!

I was looking from one to the other like I was watching a tennis match. Only, Magenta turned round and started to walk away from her chalet and, instead of going to meet her, Liam also ducked behind one of the trees that form an avenue down the middle of the row of chalets. It was like he was hiding from her as well. I wasn't sure what was going on here, but I wanted to find out.

Magenta walked past the tree where I was hiding and headed back towards the main camp. It was tricky because I had to edge round the tree trunk away from her so that she didn't see me. She walked past me without even noticing – which was good in a spying sort of way, but it hurt so much – I just wanted to reach out and touch her and tell her that I was sorry for whatever it was that I'd done to make her go off.

But things were getting spookier because, as soon as she'd got to the end of the row past the last tree, Liam sneaked out and started to follow her. He was dodging from tree, to billboard, to bus stop as he slithered his way through camp about twenty metres behind her. It didn't make sense. If she was supposed to be meeting up with him, why wasn't he walking with her? And, I must be honest, I didn't understand why Magenta didn't seem to be that bothered. It wasn't like she was looking around for him or anything. In fact, she didn't seem at all fazed that she was wandering about the place on her own at night.

So there we were, the three of us in procession: Magenta, who was picking up speed now and heading towards the chairlifts, Liam following her like some second-rate PI and then me following Liam – and I like to think that as private investigators go, I was streets ahead of the lamebrain in terms of both discretion and professionalism.

But then, out of the shadows came this weird guy that we've been seeing around camp all week – Freakshow Fred, Spud calls him. Now if anyone should've done a Prodigy tribute act, it should've been him. He has wall-to-wall tattoos, piercings in places I daren't even mention and he walks around screaming at seagulls. But Freakshow Fred started dodging round the corner of chalets and seemed to be keeping an eye on Liam, the same way Liam was keeping an eye on Magenta and I was keeping both eyes on all of them.

So there were four of us in the chain now: Magenta, Liam, Freakshow Fred and me, all sneaking along the path following each other, dipping in and out of anything that afforded us any cover. The only one who seemed oblivious to all this was Magenta, and I was beginning to suspect that maybe she wasn't planning to meet up with Liam after all – because if that had been their plan, why hadn't he just gone to her like any normal person? And if she wasn't meeting him, then where was she going and what was he doing trailing her like a stalker? And, more intriguingly, who was stalking him? I was feeling more like James Bond with every step.

As Magenta reached the cable car docking area, she put her hand out, like she was checking for rain. She was looking round idly but not in a way that made me think she was waiting to meet someone. Things were getting intriguing – very intriguing indeed.

I must admit, I was surprised that the chairlifts were still working; I'd have thought that they'd have been stopped with a thunderstorm brewing. But I couldn't even see anyone in the operating box. Magenta was waiting for the next chair to swing round – actually, they weren't so much like chairs as wooden park benches on metal supports – and as one came in from the beach and swung round the circular terminal, Magenta waited till it caught her behind the knees and sat down on it.

But then, Liam only went and leaped out of the darkness and jumped up next to her. I'm not usually into *I-told-you-so*, but – I did! And I was gutted. This was one of those times I'd have given anything to have been wrong. It was like my worst fears had just materialised in front of me. I felt like someone had rammed a red-hot poker into my chest and torn my heart apart. Another flash of lightning ripped through the sky. One, two, three, four – there it was: the deafening clap of thunder that meant the storm was getting closer. Only a mile away now.

I felt like a weight the size of a boulder had been dropped on my shoulders. I was just about to turn round and go back – I couldn't bear to watch any longer – but then something really weird happened – as the chairlift swept Magenta and Liam away down towards the beach, Freakshow Fred stepped out from behind a giant advertising board and stood in the middle of the path with his arms folded. He was staring at the cable car as it disappeared into the night, then as another chair swept round the giant wheel that propelled the chairlifts, Freakshow Fred jumped into it. But instead of sitting up like a normal person, he lay down along the seat, so that he was almost out of sight.

If there's one thing stronger than pain, it's curiosity. I didn't know what was going on, but I was sure as hell going to find out. There was a bad feeling about it all.

I started to jog along the path underneath the chairlift. It was raining heavily by now but I could still see Magenta above me and slightly ahead of me – and, I don't know if it was the light or what, but she seemed to be backing away from Liam. In fact she was backed so far away from him that she was right in the corner of the seat and was leaning over the side. Liam was leaning in towards her and the two of them were both at one side of the cable car, making it lean at a very dodgy angle. If she wasn't careful, she'd fall right out. I put a spurt on – if that did happen, I wanted to be close enough to at least have a go at catching her. As I was running beneath the chairlift, I could see the two of them. The lightning was coming so fast now that it was like watching an old black and white movie with strobe effect lighting. And the rain and the thunder were deafening. Call it a gut instinct but I knew that

Magenta needed my help. I just didn't know how to help her when she was about ten metres above my head in a cable car with a psycho.

The rain was pelting down. I was soaked. I ripped off my neck brace and tossed it to one side, then jacked it up a little. I needed to catch up with that cable car – or, better still, get to the beach before it, so that I was there, ready to snatch her away from the nutter the minute their chair docked. I was beginning to get the idea that Magenta hadn't been planning to meet up with Liam after all, but that he was coming on to her.

Then, above the noise of the rain, I heard her.

'Help!' she yelled. 'Help!'

'I'm here,' I called up to her, but another crash of thunder sounded and my words got lost in the din.

I had no choice; I legged it down the path as fast as I could until I came to the ice cream kiosk next to the terminus on the beach. It was closed at this time of night, so I hid behind it until I saw the chair descending. I could also hear Magenta's voice now above the pounding of the rain and boy, did she sound mad at him.

'What!' she screamed. 'How could you? Why would you say that? I wouldn't go within a ten-metre diving board of your lips . . .'

See – I *knew* Liam had been lying! Didn't I say, when he first told me that Magenta had been liberal with her lips, that I didn't believe him? And this time, I'm happy to say – I told you so! I can't believe I let Justine persuade me that Magenta had been unfaithful. Just wait till I see her. The chairlift was descending now and I could see and hear them clearly even though the rain was hammering on the roof of the kiosk.

'. . . not even if you were the last boy on the planet – in fact, in the entire Universe!' she was yelling at the top of her voice. 'So, back off and get back to the other end of the seat – now!'

How could I ever have believed that my Magenta was a player? Deep down, I always knew I could trust her. It felt like the concrete boulder had been lifted from my shoulders.

Then I heard Liam's mocking voice. 'Ooooooo!' he sneered. 'I'm scared.'

That was it! No one was going to treat my girl that way. I jumped out from the shadow of the ice cream hut. 'Well, you should be scared!' I shouted.

They both looked over the side of the chair.

'Daniel!' Magenta shouted. 'Help me!'

'I'm here for you,' I called back.

But just at that moment there was another flash of

lightning and a deafening crack of thunder – right overhead. The whole chairlift crackled and vibrated, then gave a sort of sizzle before it ground to a halt about three metres above the beach. Oh no! I couldn't believe it – Magenta had been struck by lightning. I felt sick. To have been so close to making up again only to see her fried in front of my eyes. I couldn't bear it.

'Magenta!' I called to her. 'Speak to me!'

'Caaaaaaaaaatch!' she yelled, as she threw herself over the side of the chairlift. I ran towards her with my arms outstretched but I was too late. She landed on all fours – splat – in the wet sand.

For the second time in two minutes I felt like a man who'd had a reprieve from the death sentence. I ran to her. 'Magenta. I love you so much.'

She stood up and brushed the sand from her knees. 'Daniel!' she said. 'I said to catch me. Now look – this is my best skirt and it's got all sand in the sequins.'

The rain had plastered her hair to her head and she looked so sweet standing there drenched. I was just about to wrap my arms round her when there was a thud from behind me as Liam jumped out of the chair on to the beach.

'So you reckon you're hard, do you?' he sneered.

He was curling the fingers of both hands in a sort of beckoning action. 'Well, bring it on then.'

'Go on, Daniel!' Magenta said. 'You show him!'

Eeek! When I'd shouted that Liam *should* be scared, it hadn't really occurred to me that I might have to back up the threat with some action.

'Come on then,' Liam laughed. Then he started playing with his bottom lip, making bub bub bub baby-noises. 'Or is the little cradle-snatcher just a big wuss.'

OK – that was it! I reached out and caught him by the hoody then spun him round to face me full on. I grabbed his shoulders and pulled him in towards me, like I used to when I went to judo. Yeah, it was all coming back to me now. As I turned my shoulder in to his chest, I put my leg in between his then pulled him over my shoulder. Bam! He landed flat on his back on the sand. I may not have been to judo for three years, but I guess it's like riding a bike – once you learn, you never forget.

'Wuss, am I? Well at least I don't get my kicks from terrorising girls.'

'Wow, Daniel! How amazing is that! I didn't realise you were so macho.'

Liam was lying on the wet sand gasping for breath – I think I must've winded him. 'Now,' I said, offering him my hand. 'I think you owe my girlfriend an apology.'

He shook his head and gasped, 'In your—'

But before he could finish there was another thud as Freakshow Fred jumped out of his chair. Uh-oh! He was coming towards us and, believe me, he did not look happy.

'Gerrup!' he barked at Liam – a bit like when he shouts at the seagulls to get out of his way.

Liam looked up. 'Dad?'

Whoa! Freakshow Fred was Liam's dad? Which went part of the way to explain why he was following him, but even so, I wouldn't expect my dad to go around stalking me – unless I was under curfew or something.

'I said – GERRUP!' Freakshow Fred ordered. 'I told you – talent show then straight to bed.'

'Yeah, but—' Liam began.

'No buts!' Fred bellowed. 'You're supposed to be in training. Now get back to bed! You've got t'World Championships in a couple of weeks and you're gallivanting about terrorising little girls.'

'Hey,' Magenta protested. 'Less of the *little*. I'll be fourteen in two days. In fact, when I think about it, it's actually less than two . . .'

Her voice trailed away as Freakshow Fred

ignored her and carried on laying into his son. 'It's bad enough you've messed up your training schedule this week. Getting yourself banned from t'high platform . . .'

Magenta leaned towards me and whispered, 'High platform? Is he talking shoes or train stations?'

'I might be shooting from the hip here, but I think he's talking diving boards.'

Liam was pointing at Magenta. 'I told you – that was all *her* fault. She was coming on to me and she lied about her age and then she was larking about on the boards. It was all her fault I got banned from the pool. I was just getting my own back.'

'Ex! Cuse! Me!' Uh-oh! I took Magenta by the shoulder and led her towards the path back up to the camp before she got embroiled in Liam's family argument.

'Let's leave Liam and his dad to sort this out, shall we?'

'OK, so maybe he had a point with the thing about the age, but I only added a week – he was the one who added a whole year,' she explained as we walked back up the path. 'And, hello! *Me* coming on to *him*? I don't think so! Did you see the way he was flirting with me – oh no – I forgot, you were playing piggyback with Justine in the pool . . .' OK, so now it was all crystal clear. *That's* what I'd done to upset her. '. . . and as for getting him banned from the pool, honestly, Daniel, it seemed to have slipped his mind that he was the homicidal maniac who had me dangling three metres above the water. Talk about not taking responsibility . . .'

'Shhh!' I put my finger to her lips and pulled her towards me. 'We're going to put this whole week behind us – right?'

'OK but—'

Before she could say anything else, I kissed her. Right there on the footpath outside the donkey stables. The thunder was trailing off into the distance and the rain was splashing gently on our heads and running down our faces, but I didn't care. I'd got my Magenta back. And wow! Talk about saving the best till last!

Magenta

Did I have the best birthday ever! I knew being fourteen would be worth it.

But before I tell you about my party – which was a sleepover by the way – with boys! I mean, how open-minded is my dad these days? I give all the credit to Belinda of course. There's no way he would've allowed that without her. I'm soooo pleased that my stepmother didn't turn out to be one of those evil ones who make their stepdaughters scrub the floors and do all the work like you hear about in fairy tales.

Of course there were girls at my sleepover too. Arlette and Seema were both back from their holidays, which was soooo brilliant to see them again. It's been ages since we saw each other. And Hattie Pringle and Chelsea Riordan were there, as well as Candy Meekin.

But before I tell you about it, there was masses more happened before we even got to that.

  1) Freakshow Fred only brought Liam to our room on the last morning as we were packing up to

leave and made him apologise for scaring me and spreading rumours about me. Which was only fair, I thought. It turns out that because he blamed me for ruining his training schedule in the run-up to the World Championships, he decided to ruin my holiday too. Nice boy – not!

2) Daniel had a go at Justine for also spreading nasty things about me and she went off in a sulk. But the good side of that is that she told Auntie Heather that she wanted to go straight home from the camp rather than come back here for my party – yay! Suits me just fine.

3) Sadly, Spud's talent show entry had been less like breakdancing and more like break-necking. He ended up like half of our group – in a surgical collar. I can't help feeling I missed out somehow.

But worst of all,

4) We were just about to set off home when Mary, Daniel's mum, rang him. It seems that she and Donald had come home early and found that, when Holden had been cleaning his teeth before we set off, he'd only gone and left the tap running – ooops! Their whole house was flooded. But the best bit is, Daniel's family have got to move in with us! How amazing is that?

Only till the insurance is sorted out, obviously, but till then, Daniel's going to be sleeping in my bed. Of course, I'll have to share with Gran, which is a bit of a downer, and Mary and Donald are going to be camping out in the sitting room once the party's over. But how fantastic will it be to have Daniel as a house-mate? Am I the luckiest girl in the world or what?

Anyway, to get back to my party – it was brilliant! You should've seen Daniel. Oh, he looked so gorgeous. Now that he's out of his collar, he looks sooooo cute. He's got a suntanned face and body but this paler stripe from his chin to his collar bone where the sun couldn't reach because of his neck brace – sweet. The Lyle twins came, and you should've heard Daniel talking to them about Liam – he was amazing. He was trying to big himself up and be all macho.

'I was like a ninja. Thwack! Down he went on to the sand . . .'

I went all gooey inside when I heard him – it was so sweet the way he was telling them about rescuing me. I felt really special. In fact, I felt special the whole day – and night. It was way better than I could ever have imagined.

And you should've seen what Daniel gave me as a present.

'Shut your eyes,' he said to me. I could feel him putting something round my neck – and it didn't feel like it was made out of foam either – which had got to be a relief! 'Now open them.' He was holding a mirror up for me and there was this gorgeous silver locket in the shape of a heart. Wow! It was beautiful – and soooooo sophisticated. 'It's antique,' he explained, opening the little catch on the side. 'And look inside.'

Oh my God! He'd only gone and printed out the picture from his phone of the two of us kissing (it's the one he has as the display) and put it in one side of the locket – how romantic is that? And, I don't know much about antiques, but I'm thinking it must've cost him masses of pocket money too. Am I the luckiest girl in the world or what?

We put our sleeping bags right at the far side of the room near the window, so that we could still watch the DVDs but also have some privacy. And we talked and cuddled up ALL NIGHT! How adult are we?

But everyone's gone now. Well, almost. The only ones left are the ones who are staying here – Mary,

Donald and Daniel. We were all sitting round having breakfast – you see, now Daniel and I can even hold hands over the muesli – when Dad cleared his throat like he was going to make a speech or something.

'Well, it's been an eventful week for everyone,' he said.

Ha! He could say that again, considering we'd had:

- Five life-threatening incidents,
- Four neck braces,
- Three police involvements,
- Two birthdays
- And a donkey in a bedroom!

'But,' he went on, 'I want to thank you all for making it such a wonderful holiday.' Huh? Did I miss something? He was at the same holiday camp as me, right? But he was grinning like he meant it and he had his arm round Belinda's shoulder. 'I've got some good news . . . sorry, *we've* got some good news.' They gave each other this gooey smile, then he said, 'Belinda's pregnant!'

Oh my God! Belinda had this grin on her face like she'd just won some organic lotto for world peace or something and Gran and Mary were both hugging her. Donald shook Dad's hand like he was awarding him a prize.

Daniel squeezed me and gave me this great big kiss. 'Congratulations! You're going to be the best big sister ever.'

And he was right. I *am* going to be the best big sister ever. Oh my God! This was the best birthday present in the world.

I'm going to be a role model! Yay! I can't wait!

A note from the author

Most of Magenta's antics are based on things that have happened in real life (I just stretch them a bit for dramatic effect) and Shades of Magenta is no different. In my work as an author I visit lots of schools and, last summer, a boy told me of an incident when he'd been on holiday to Cornwall and come back to their cottage to find a donkey on his bed. It was such a funny image that I knew I had to use it. So thank you Shahazad for inspiring me.